Jac X
Jacobs, Nancy Baker,
Star struck : a Quinn
Collins mystery $ 25.95

Star Struck

Other Five Star Titles by Nancy Baker Jacobs:

Double or Nothing

Star Struck

A Quinn Collins Mystery

Nancy Baker Jacobs

Five Star • Waterville, Maine

Copyright © 2002 by Nancy Baker Jacobs

All rights reserved.

This novel is a work of fiction. Names, characters, places and incidents are either the product of the author's imagination, or, if real, used fictitiously.

Five Star First Edition Mystery Series.

Published in 2002 in conjunction with Tekno-Books and Ed Gorman.

Set in 11 pt. Plantin by Minnie B. Raven.

Printed in the United States on permanent paper.

Library of Congress Cataloging-in-Publication Data

Jacobs, Nancy Baker, 1944–
Star struck : a Quinn Collins mystery / Nancy Baker Jacobs.
p. cm.—(Five Star first edition mystery series)
ISBN 0-7862-4171-3 (hc : alk. paper)
1. Hollywood (Los Angeles, Calif.)—Fiction. 2. Motion picture industry—Fiction. 3. Women journalists—Fiction. I. Title. II. Series.
PS3560.A2554 S73 2002
813′.54—dc21 2002023268

Star Struck

1

I arrived in Malibu on that spring morning ten minutes too early for my interview with Shane King. And far too late.

The morning's fog was just beginning to burn off as I reached the young movie mogul's beach house for my nine o'clock appointment. The wrought-iron gates at the street entrance to the grounds were standing open, so I drove on through and parked in the circular driveway. The sea gulls were particularly noisy here above the beach this morning, swooping and scolding, then landing on the red tile roof of the low stucco house and screeching at each other. The only other sound was that of the waves hitting the shoreline below the bluff. As I turned off my engine, I debated whether to wait out those ten minutes in my car or to go ahead and ring the doorbell.

The interview with Shane King here at his beach house was the last one I needed for my article on "baby moguls," the fuzz-faced youths who hold so many power positions in today's entertainment industry. I'm Quinn Collins, reporter for the *Hollywood Star*, a show business trade publication that competes with *Variety* and *The Hollywood Reporter*. The *Star*'s a weekly, while the others are dailies, so we try to provide a more in-depth, analytical look at the entertainment business than our competition. There are fewer canned press releases in the *Hollywood Star*, more features and trend analyses. I'd planned this current feature to profile nearly a dozen movers and shakers under thirty, all of whom were well on their way to power and riches.

I'd already had one session with Shane King, a few days earlier at his Calistoga Pictures office. At only twenty-three, he was an executive vice president. Yet, from what I'd observed in my first interview, young Shane demonstrated no particular aptitude for his job, assuming he even understood what it was supposed to be. His qualifications seemed to include nothing more than his blond surfer-boy good looks and his youth. Plus, undoubtedly, some very good connections. I wanted Shane in my article despite his lack of visible aptitude for moviemaking; he seemed the perfect symbol of the way the movie industry worships youth at the expense of talent and maturity.

I had to admit that the negative angle I'd tentatively decided to pursue on Shane was giving me a touch of indigestion. Not because he deserved coddling. Hell, the kid was pulling down more than a quarter of a million bucks a year for doing nothing I could readily identify. That made him fair game. No, it was my long past relationship with Shane's father, Peter, that was gnawing at me this early in the day. I'd had a brief but rather torrid affair with Peter King almost twenty years earlier, when I was a naive twenty-four-year-old, not-very-successful actress and he, at thirty-five, was nearing the peak of his directing career. Peter had had those blond surfer good looks once, too. Along with a few other things I still found appealing.

I hadn't laid eyes on Peter for at least seven years now, not since I'd attended his older son's funeral—hardly an occasion on which to rekindle passion. Nowadays, Peter was having a hard time, struggling to get directing work on low budget features and television dramas, while his younger son, who'd been only two years old when we were dating, was in fat city. In the crazy world of show people, that pretty much amounted to business as usual.

I sat in my old Mercedes for a moment and looked around the place. The garage door was open, revealing a brand new dark green Jaguar parked inside. Shane had good taste, all right, expensive taste. His house was definitely in millionaire territory, too—three thousand square feet of white stucco, steel, and glass perched on stilts above the sand, a very impressive engineering feat. The graceful arches along the front of the wide, red-tile-roofed building were thick with magenta bougainvillea that provided a vivid contrast with the pristine white stucco and the varied blues of the sky and sea. To my right was a large rock garden landscaped with succulent plants, blue flowering lilies of the Nile, and a gurgling white marble fountain; a stream of water spouted from the mouth of the small stone boy at the fountain's center into the shallow pool at his feet.

The stretch of beach on which Shane King's house stood was farther away from Los Angeles than the famous Malibu Colony, and it wasn't quite as prestigious, but certainly none of the houses on this short street would sell for less than four million dollars.

Fat salary or not, I felt certain that Shane didn't own this impressive place. He had to be renting it, probably for at least seven or eight grand a month. He'd probably leased his Jag as well.

My guess was that it was all a good investment, though. In Hollywood, one lesson everyone learns early is that appearances are everything. The right address is often worth its highway-robbery price, if only because half the battle in getting hired in show business is looking like you don't need the work. Most of the Rolls Royces and Mercedes and Jaguars in this town are leased by people who could never afford to own them. And I've known lots of ambitious folks who stretched their finances beyond all reasonable limits so they could live in the "right" ZIP code. Yet their mansions in Beverly Hills, Bel Air, and Malibu were nearly empty inside. Their credit cards simply wouldn't stretch far enough to cover furnishing those pricey digs.

Luckily, show biz journalists aren't held to the same standards as others working in the business. Our power lies in the influence we have, not in the money we earn. My Mercedes was twelve years old—not old enough to be a classic and far too old to be in fashion. Although I could afford a newer car, I kept this one because I liked it; it ran with precision and I saw no need to change. I didn't need a trendy address, either. Since I'd sold my house, I'd been living in the guesthouse on my uncle Teddy's Pacific Palisades property. That was a long, long way from the slums, but my little piece of paradise was both compact and borrowed.

By the time I'd finished my visual survey of Shane King's status symbols, the clock on the Mercedes' dashboard told me it was two minutes to nine. Close enough, I decided, grabbing my tape recorder and notebook and climbing out of the car. I crossed under the hanging bougainvillea and rang the bell at the front door, listening to its chime echoing inside the house. A gray-and-white sea gull landed on the front steps beside me and began to scold loudly.

"Do I look like breakfast to you?" I asked him, annoyed. The gull squawked at me again. "Get lost!" I swung my shoulder bag in the fat bird's direction and he fluttered his wings, then flew upward and landed half a dozen feet away, eyeing me quizzically. The early morning hours never had been my best, particularly when I'd been covering a screening and party for Jodie Foster's latest picture until almost two o'clock the night before. Nice work, of course, rubbing elbows with movers and shakers, but it *was* work. Sheer fatigue tended to make me cranky, at least until around midday, when my adrenaline resumed flowing.

I rang the doorbell again and peered through the small rectangular glass insert in the front door. All I could see through this thick piece of glass was a portion of the living room, which was furnished completely in overstuffed white linen, along with a flash of grayish blue beyond—the sea shining through the wide wall of glass at the back of the house. A massive modern oil painting in vibrant blues and greens hung over the fireplace at the north end of the room. I had no idea what the painting was supposed to represent; it reminded me of the cracked bottom of my uncle's swimming pool. Still, my bet was that it had cost a small fortune.

I looked at my watch and began to steam. It was exactly nine o'clock. Keeping people waiting was another common Hollywood power trick; self-important people did it to let you know their time was far more valuable than yours. Stupid power game or not, I resented it, particularly at the hands of a twenty-three-year-old I'd known nearly since he was in diapers. Particularly when I was making do with four hours of sleep. Despite my fatigue, I had still managed to show up as promised. It didn't seem too much to ask that the subject of my interview do the same.

Who did Shane King think he was, anyway? I told myself he ought to be blessing me and the *Hollywood Star* for all the free publicity we were about to give him, then thrust my finger against the doorbell a third time, harder this time. The chimes echoed once more, but still no one came to the door. Obviously, Shane hadn't been able to stretch his fat paycheck far enough to hire household help. That petty observation made me feel only slightly better.

I started back toward my car, fuming. If I waited, Shane

King would probably wander to the door in fifteen minutes, maybe half an hour, wearing a bathrobe and claiming he'd been in the shower at nine o'clock and hadn't heard the doorbell. I was tempted to leave, to write my article using only the information I'd already gathered. Maybe I would even include a sharp dig about Shane King's not showing up for his second interview with the *Star*, teach the young snot a lesson about showing some respect for the press.

But that little bit of revenge would also leave me with a half-baked story. I reminded myself that I was a professional journalist, not another insecure film land wannabe. Not only that, but ever since last summer, when the *Hollywood Star* hit hard financial times, I'd been a part owner. I'd sold my house in Santa Monica just as real estate prices began to recover for the first time since the '94 earthquake. Then I'd invested most of the cash I got for it in the newspaper. Now, I felt even more responsibility for making the *Star* successful—however much it might wound my pride.

By the time I had my car door halfway open, I was beginning to cool down, to rationalize a bit for Shane, to find a way to excuse and forgive his rude behavior. I'm not good at waiting, but I'm even less good at staying angry for long, even with people who deserve it. I get mightily furious, all right, but in the end, I have to confess I almost never do a whole lot about it. It's not so much that I wimp out; it's just that I have a short attention span. Before long, I'm onto something else, forgetting all about such petty slights.

Once, for instance, a notoriously difficult and equally famous actor made me travel all the way to Denver, where he was shooting a picture, for an interview. Then he kept me waiting in the hot sun for two days, until, as he put it, "the vibes were right" for him to talk to me. That long-awaited event took place shortly before midnight on the second night, after the actor had consumed an entire fifth of scotch. I swallowed my pride, did the interview while fending off his drunken sexual advances, and vowed never to give the bastard a line of print in the *Hollywood Star* again. Yet, when I ran into him at the next year's Academy Awards show, I was swept up in the moment and completely forgot my promise to myself. I quickly scheduled another interview. Luckily, this time, the aging pretty-boy was a pussycat. I guess he figured the vibes were better the second time around. Or maybe he'd discovered AA.

It was probably just as well that I seldom got around to dumping my ire on people. You never know when something you've said in anger is going to come back to haunt you. One thing about Hollywood—there's always somebody power tripping you, putting you down so they can be up. I've always had to endure directors who don't return my phone calls until I've rung them ten or fifteen times; actors who "forget" to mail me invitations to important cocktail parties, forcing me to crash the gates; even rival reporters who bad-mouth me to their sources as they angle for exclusives. One thing about being a show business journalist—you have to develop the hide of a rhinoceros and the sensitivities of a snake if you're going to get your stories.

Even after so many years as a reporter covering this oddball beat, I was still learning that lesson.

Maybe Shane was out on his back deck, or sunning himself on the beach below, I told myself. Perhaps he honestly had never expected me to be on time for our appointment. Lord knows nobody—except, of course, the news media and the desperate—ever arrives anywhere on time in this town. I decided to poke around here a bit, to give Shane King the benefit of the doubt. I would use the young mogul's tardiness as an excuse to snoop around his property until he decided to show up for our meeting. As long as he did that in the next half hour. A half hour was my limit. After that, I was out of there.

There was nothing but a narrow, sturdy fence on the south side of the house, between Shane's garage and the garage of the property next door, a massive white house with neogothic pillars across the front—a pretentious imitation Tara-at-the-beach. Beyond the fence, I could see the hazy outline of an oil tanker heading north as it slowly crossed the horizon. I spun around and headed toward the north side of the house. There, I found a narrow stone pathway behind a flowering camellia bush; the flagstones led me around the side of the house, where I climbed four concrete steps to a redwood walkway and followed it around to a large deck at the back of the house.

The view from here was spectacular, even with what remained of the morning's fog diffusing the coastline. At night, Santa Monica's "queen's necklace" would be visible from this spot. The name derives from the curve of the coastline; in the dark, the lights of the buildings along the shoreline resemble a string of dazzling diamonds. Sunsets from this venue had to be dazzling, too. I revised my estimate upward; Shane King might well be shelling out nine or even ten grand a month to rent this place.

I ran my finger lightly across the surface of the round, glass-topped patio table on the deck. It came up wet. The plastic mesh chairs and the redwood decking were soaked as well, almost as if it had rained during the night. Yet I knew it hadn't; this moisture was simply the result of the season's daily fog. I peered through thick sliding glass doors into the living room, examining the other side of the same room I'd seen from the front door. I could see more from here—a glass-top, iron-legged coffee table with a selection of magazines laid out across its top, and another modernistic painting, this one vaguely reminiscent of nude lovers lying on the sand—but I still detected no signs of life.

As I progressed along the deck, I became aware of a faint vibration beneath my feet. I looked over the railing at the beach below, but the tide was low; the waves were not hitting against the pillars that held up the house. The rumbling motion of the deck had to be coming from some other source, perhaps a generator or a water pump, I thought.

Next to the living room, I found a massive bathroom with its own sliding glass door to the outdoors. I spotted a sunken tub and a glassed-in shower, along with the requisite toilet and bidet. The tile floor and walls were stark white, and fluffy black-and-white striped towels hung with sharp precision on three racks along the walls. There were full-length curtains in this room, but they hadn't been drawn. The fact was that, unless somebody like me was out here on the deck spying, nobody would be able to see into this bathroom. Nobody who wasn't somewhere out on the water with a pair of strong binoculars, anyway. The angle of sight from the beach below was wrong, and the only close neighbors were in the house on the south side. Someone bathing in that tub could soak for hours and enjoy the view at the same time, in near-complete privacy.

I was beginning to feel like a voyeur, but this was hardly the first time I'd felt that way; in my job, I'd had to get used to snooping. A large bedroom was next in line along the back of the house. Here long, creamy white draperies were pulled across the floor-to-ceiling windows, all except for a foot or so in the center where they didn't quite meet.

I reassured myself that I had nothing to be ashamed of. After all, Shane King had now kept me waiting a good fifteen minutes past our specified interview time, and I was merely researching my story in his absence. The vibration beneath my feet grew stronger and I prayed that it wasn't the start of another earthquake as I moved slowly toward the gap in the curtains.

Because of the partially closed drapes, this room was darker than the others. Still, I could see it wasn't kept nearly as neatly as the rest of the house. There were a pair of jeans and a blue sweater thrown across a chair near the window, and I noticed a white leather athletic shoe lying on the eggshell carpet near it. My eyes followed a trail of castoff clothing—a blue-and-white striped shirt and a pair of rumpled white sweat socks—toward the bed, which was a huge circle covered with a black-and-white zebra-print bedspread. Hardly my taste in bedding, but probably very expensive, and certainly the kind of thing that was popular with Hollywood's young bachelor set.

Opposite the bed, I discovered the source of the deck's rumbling motion. In the corner of the room, directly beneath a skylight that illuminated it clearly, was a rectangular Jacuzzi with steam rising from the surface of its churning, bubbling water. But it was what was perched against one corner of the spa that held my eye. A young man lay back against its smooth acrylic surface, his face tilted slightly upward toward the light and one arm dangling over the side. The recognizable thatch of sun-streaked dark blond hair on his head told me this was Shane King.

My anger and frustration began to surface once more. So this was where the little bastard was hiding, I thought. Here he was, relaxing in his Jacuzzi, completely ignoring his appointment with me as though I were some nobody who'd been begging him for favors. I knocked sharply on the glass door and tried to slide it open, but it was securely locked. I began to pound on it. "Shane King!" I called, "open this door."

He didn't move. I knocked on the glass again, then shaded my eyes from the glare with my hands and pressed my forehead against the glass. Now I could see that Shane's eyes were wide open. I kicked at the bottom of the doorframe, rattling the glass, but he didn't blink. Despite the morning sun's warming the air around me, a chill began to crawl slowly down my spine.

I knocked again, much more lightly this time, by now knowing it would do no good. Knocking on the window was merely something to do while I processed my thoughts. A vision of Shane King's older brother in his casket five years ago flashed before my eyes. Rhett King had been only nineteen or twenty when he died. Now Peter King's second son—

Unless Shane wasn't really dead, I thought, grasping for some other explanation, any other explanation. Could this be some kind of joke? Could this be Shane's way of frightening me, of punishing me because I'd been snooping around his property while he'd been trying to avoid me? But I didn't really believe that.

I knew that the best I could hope for was that the young man inside was only comatose, not dead. Maybe he'd merely passed out from being immersed too long in the hot water. If I got help quickly enough, maybe he could still be saved.

I sprinted back around to the front of the house as fast as I could, grabbed my cell phone out of my car's glove compartment, and dialed 911.

Then I paced the circular driveway while I waited for help to show up. The faster I paced, the more I shivered. I hoped against hope that I wouldn't be attending another funeral soon, and prayed that I wouldn't have to extend my condolences once more to Peter King.

I couldn't think of a single thing I'd ever be able to say to comfort him.

2

Within minutes, the circular driveway was filled with emergency vehicles. But the paramedics couldn't save Shane King. They told me he'd probably been dead for several hours by the time I arrived. Now an investigation was underway to determine exactly what had happened to this twenty-three-year-old who'd had everything going for him.

I sat on the front steps of the beach house, holding my head in my hands. The gull came back again, approaching me tentatively. This time I didn't bother shooing him away. I didn't have the energy.

"Hey, Quinn," a low male voice growled at me. "Quinn Collins."

I looked up to see Detective Tracy Lewis's round fifty-year-old face smiling down at me. "Hello, Tracy." I was relieved that Detective Lewis had been the one to catch this call. Somehow his presence made my finding a dead body just a touch more bearable. Our paths had crossed several times in recent months—while I was researching a feature on show people who'd lost their homes in the latest round of fires in Malibu, then again when I did a similar story on the mud slides that followed. We'd had coffee together a couple of times, comparing war stories and sharing the adrenaline-rush excitement that always surrounds a natural disaster. He was a likable guy.

Lewis brushed away a few bougainvillea petals and sat down beside me. "What exactly brought you out here so bright and early?"

Funny, I thought, that I wasn't feeling any adrenaline rush around this particular disaster. This time, much more than mere property had been lost, and all I felt was exhaustion, depression. "I had a nine o'clock appointment here to interview Shane," I explained. "What happened to him?"

Lewis pushed a shock of gray-streaked mahogany hair off his forehead. "Looks like a drug overdose."

"But that's imposs—" I swallowed my words. Not two days earlier, Shane King had flashed his baby blues in my direction and assured me that he never, ever touched illegal drugs. He'd vowed that what had happened to his older brother would never happen to him, and I'd believed him. Despite having lived my whole life armpit-deep in Hollywood bullshit, sometimes I can still be surprisingly naive. "Shane told me he'd never been a user," I said, feeling a little foolish. "He—He didn't look like one and, after what happened to Rhett, I figured—"

Lewis's eyes rolled skyward behind his gold-rimmed glasses. "Yeah, right. The kid didn't use. And that sea gull over there doesn't crap on the sand, either. Hell, Quinn, you and I both know half the people in show business are high on something most of the time—booze, if nothing else. And all of them liars. Goes with the territory."

I wasn't quite as cynical as the good detective. The truth was that, despite all its warts, despite the way it attracts world-class phonies and neurotics, I still loved show business. I simply couldn't envision myself working in any other industry. One thing about Hollywood—it was never dull. And what has always driven me craziest is dullness, routine, predictability. I crave the adrenaline rush change always gives me. Hell, I'll settle for chaos over calm any day. "So Shane lied," I said. "What was he using?"

"We'll have to analyze what was in the syringe we found

on the floor tiles next to the Jacuzzi, but my guess is it'll be cocaine. Or maybe heroin. It's made a real comeback, especially with the kids." He stretched his legs out straight in front of him. "Let's hear what you planned to see Shane King about."

I told Detective Tracy Lewis about my article, including my interview with Shane at Calistoga Pictures. I did not, however, mention my long-ago relationship with Shane's dad.

"So the big brother OD'd, too," Lewis said, shaking his head fiercely, as though he was angry, involved in some internal argument. "Christ, there's so many of them, it's hard to keep track anymore."

"It happened about seven years ago," I said. "Rhett King was nineteen or twenty when he died." I remembered meeting Rhett just once, when he was around six. His hair was so light it was nearly white, and the grin on his dimpled face whenever his busy dad found time to spend a few hours with him could break your heart.

"Goddamned spoiled brats." I flinched at the vehemence behind Lewis's words. "Kid like this one—he gets everything just handed to him, and what does he do with it? Shoots poison into his veins and checks out!" With a loud sigh, he pulled himself back to his job and took a notebook and pencil out of the inside pocket of his sport coat. "I need to take down your statement about finding the body," he said, matter-of-factly. "Later, I'll have it typed up and you can sign it."

I told him everything that had happened since my arrival here at ten minutes before nine. "You're really certain Shane was already dead by then?" I asked.

"Looks that way. Why?"

"Just—Well, I'd hate to think if I'd just broken in, if I

knew CPR or something—Well, you know."

"Don't worry about it, Quinn. There wasn't a god-damned thing you could've done. The kid was long gone."

I pulled my own notebook and pencil out of my purse, reminding myself that, like Lewis, I had a job to do here. Shane King's unexpected death had changed its nature, that was all. "Okay if I quote you on the suspected overdose?" I asked.

"I don't want you printing this yet, Quinn," he told me. "I still have to wait for the coroner's people to show up here, then I have to go notify the kid's next of kin. I don't want those poor people reading about this before I get a chance to talk to them. And I don't want you calling them up, bugging them for quotes before I reach them, either."

"Come on, Tracy, lighten up. The *Hollywood Star*'s a weekly and my deadline's not until Thursday noon. That gives you plenty of time to locate Shane King's family."

I didn't much want to talk with the young man's parents, anyway. That promised to be far too painful a conversation, and I feared I was too involved to be objective. Tracy Lewis needn't have worried; the last task I wanted to take upon myself was being first to tell Peter and Veronica King that their son was dead. I gladly relinquished that job to him.

I was pretty sure, however, that when I talked to him at Calistoga Pictures, Shane had told me he had a girlfriend. I made a mental note to listen to my tape of our interview when I got back to the office, to find out the girl's name. I wanted to talk to Shane's lover before I wrote anything about his death; if she was willing, she could probably give me the straight story about his drug use.

Lewis sighed long and loud, as though there was something about the sheer waste of Shane King's death, and his brother's before him, that meant something more to this veteran cop than just another overdose. "Check back with me tomorrow," he told me, pushing himself up off the steps. Another bright pink petal drifted downward from the bougainvillea, landing on his graying mahogany hair. He swatted it away as though it was a pesky bee. "I'll see if there's anything else I can give you then. Your statement should be ready for you to sign tomorrow, too." Tracy Lewis's whole body seemed to slump; he was the picture of dejection.

I knew how the detective felt. I'd covered lots of show business deaths in my time, the last days of people far better known and more talented than Shane King ever would have been. There'd been the legends, people like Lucille Ball, Fred Astaire, Laurence Olivier, Vincent Price, but they'd lived long, fruitful lives and their times had come. Nowadays, however, it seemed I was being called upon more and more frequently to chronicle the life of someone struck down in the bloom of youth—those dead far too early of AIDS, and the equally senseless deaths of entertainers like River Phoenix, John Belushi, and Kurt Cobain. The fallout of drug addictions and experimentation. The tragic waste of life made me want to cry.

At only twenty-three, Shane King had had such potential. But he'd blown it all for a cheap, quick high. I was more than grateful that it was Tracy and not me who would have to break the news to his family.

As I left Shane King's house, I noticed a *Hollywood Reporter* car turning into his street and recognized the journalist at the wheel. I knew the rest of the news media wouldn't be far behind. Tracy Lewis would have much more than the *Star* to keep at bay if he wanted to suppress news of the young movie executive's death for very long.

I drove south on Pacific Coast Highway in a kind of daze. I'd just found my first corpse and the fact that death up close and personal was a whole lot different than in the movies was sinking in fast. No blood and gore here, but this was reality. Shane King was no actor playing dead in a hot tub, waiting for the director to yell, "Cut!" Shane couldn't dry himself off, toss off his fictional character, and play another role another day. This was the real thing, death without frills. This was permanent.

I stopped at a red light at the intersection of PCH and Malibu Canyon Road, just below the white stucco campus of conservative Pepperdine University. The school's location in a million-dollar neighborhood and its rolling green lawns carved from the Southern California desert spoke volumes about the affluence of its backers. My cell phone rang just as the light turned green. I grabbed it and announced, "Quinn Collins."

"Hi, Quinn, it's me," my secretary, Lucy, replied. "Glad I caught you. Wanted to let you know Henry Fong cancelled again, so no need to rush back."

My mind raced for a few seconds before what Lucy was telling me made sense. With the stress of the morning's events, I'd nearly forgotten that I had an afternoon appointment with Henry Fong in Century City. I'd been trying to interview the international financier for my Asian movie investments story for the past three weeks, and this was the fourth appointment he'd cancelled. "What else is new," I said with a sigh. Obviously, the man was less than anxious to talk to a reporter from the *Hollywood Star.* Or maybe he simply had something against big blondes. That I was secretly relieved not to have to deal with another interview on this bleak day was entirely beside the point. "Did Fong reschedule?" I asked.

"Tuesday at two—his office—if you can make it."

"Anything on my calendar?"

"Nope, it's clean." Lucy's voice on the phone began to break up as I approached the shopping center near the Malibu Colony. As usual, the parking lot of the supermarket on my right held more expensive cars than the average Mercedes Benz dealership. As the static blasted my ear, I passed the Malibu Pier. The black-scarred hill on my left was a bleak reminder of the last big brush fire. A few of the burned houses were still in ruins, but most were now being rebuilt. Soon they would cling precariously to the steep, sandy terrain once more and their owners could go back to worrying about mudslides, should heavy rains come before the hillside vegetation rejuvenated.

I held the phone away from my ear to keep the increasingly loud bursts of static from breaking my eardrum and began to shout. I tried to ignore the driver of the old Ford on my right, who shot me a look of sheer contempt. I don't even feel all that conspicuous using my car phone anymore; most of the cars on the road have them.

"Okay, Lucy," I yelled, "confirm Tuesday, but let Fong know I'll go with what I've already got if he cancels on me again. He's not going to like looking like he's running some kind of scam, trading green cards for movie financing or whatever the hell he's pulling, and—" The line hiccuped and went dead. Oh well, I thought, I'd be back at the office shortly. I could talk to Lucy there.

I skipped lunch and went directly back to the *Hollywood Star*'s offices, on Wilshire Boulevard in Santa Monica, just a few blocks east of the ocean bluff. My partners weren't in—Lucy told me that Harry was out making a few last minute advertising sales calls before this week's edition went to bed, and Bebe had an appointment with the printer. The Radners had started the *Star* more than twenty years ago, but the last couple of years had been the roughest financially. Both Harry and Bebe were hustling new advertisers and subscribers almost every waking minute. Only one of the *Star*'s other two reporters was in and she was phoning her sources for her gossip column.

I took the stack of snail mail, e-mail, faxes, and phone messages that Lucy handed me—my day's ration of news releases from publicists—and perched on the corner of her desk. I was too shaken to go right to work, so I told Lucy what I'd found at Shane King's beach house. Characteristically, she was wiping her eyes before I'd finished. Lucy Flint is in her late fifties, gray-haired and portly and completely reliable. She has a mind like a steel trap and the heart of a social worker still years away from burnout. Five years ago, as the impoverished widow of a set construction foreman who died of a heart attack, she was visibly grateful when the *Hollywood Star* gave her a chance to run our office, despite her lack of documented work experience. In all that time, she's never even called in sick. "The poor kid," Lucy said. "The poor kid. To be struck down so young—"

According to the cops, I reminded her, Shane had had the major hand in striking himself down. Which, in some ways, was even more tragic than if he'd died as the result of some dread disease or a random accident. After comforting the obviously distressed Lucy, who'd never even met the King family, I took advantage of the rare relative quiet in the office. I asked her to hold my calls and closed the door to my cubicle.

To keep my sanity, I'd always tried to do my writing at home whenever I could. My quiet little guesthouse, nestled at the back of my Uncle Teddy's Pacific Palisades property, made a much more cheerful workplace than the *Star*'s shabby office suite did.

I started writing Shane King's obituary, but found my hands shaking on the computer's keyboard, so I spent a few minutes going through my stack of news releases. It was the same old crap, usually good for a laugh.

A virtually unknown actress had opened a new shopping center in Ontario. Her publicist had sent me a selection of black-and-white photos of her, wearing an evening dress in the harsh noontime sunlight as she cut the ribbon on what looked like a generic mini-mall. A small production company announced that it was negotiating with Tom Cruise to star in the remake of a classic western. Cruise hadn't actually signed with them, of course. I recognized this press release as a trial balloon. With enough publicity about the pending "deal" with Tom Cruise, some gullible investor might actually write a check. After it was cashed, the producers would likely announce that Cruise had a conflict in his busy schedule. Then they would sign the much cheaper actor they'd intended to use all along.

A faxed quarterly report told me that Michael Eisner's pay had risen again. Not to mention his share of the Disney empire's stock options. Apparently the industry's inherent ageism wasn't reaching into all the higher echelons.

So what else was new? And did anybody really care anymore? With a pang of regret for all the dead trees this stack of paper represented, I relegated most of it to the recycle bin and turned back to my computer. If I couldn't face writing Shane King's obituary just yet—luckily, I had until Thursday to work up my courage—at least I could put in some work on my baby moguls story.

I called up what I'd already written about the youngsters in the Hollywood power structure on my computer, then deleted my references to Shane in the body of the story. I added a short paragraph about the young Calistoga Pictures executive's untimely death, marking it to run as a side bar to the main article and adding a note to readers that a more complete obituary notice could be found on the obit page. I included six other studio executives and four hot producer-directors under the age of thirty in my main story, certainly enough to illustrate my point. When I finished my article, I filed it with the rest of this week's edition, then returned four phone calls from press agents who'd assured Lucy they had urgent news for me. Finally, I felt calm enough to write Shane's obit.

Setting out the bare facts was easy enough. Shane King was born in 1978, attended Palisades High School and spent a couple of years at USC, and worked briefly as an executive at Calistoga Pictures. Then he died. I left out the official cause for now. My story was short. Shane's life simply hadn't lasted long enough for him to amass much of a biography. As for Shane's survivors, I knew they included his father, Peter King, and his mother, Veronica. Her latest husband was Joshua Meyers, the producer, but I wasn't sure whether Veronica had taken his last name or not. And I didn't know whether Veronica had had other children—who, of course, would be Shane's half-brothers and half-sisters—with the two husbands who had followed Peter. The mortuary would have that information. I made myself a note to find out where the body would be sent after the coroner's office was finished with it.

With my preliminary copy still glowing on my computer screen, I listened once more to the tape I'd made two days earlier, concentrating on the part where I'd talked to Shane about Rhett.

"Look, Ms. Collins, uh, Quinn—" I heard his youthful

voice telling me, "my brother was a good guy and I loved him a lot. I guess you could say we were pretty close most of the time, but—"

"But what?"

"Well, the truth is Rhett wasn't very tough. Took life too fucking serious. Once he started letting things get to him, he made some real dumb choices."

"You mean like his escape into drugs?" I'd prompted.

"Yeah, that sorta shit and—" There was a long pause on the tape. I out-waited Shane. "Yeah, sure, drugs," he said, finally. "I'll never touch that shit as long as I live—no way, Jose. Rhett fucked himself up royally." There was another pause, then a plaintive question—"Why the hell couldn't that stupid asshole just hang in there for once?"

I'd thought at the time Shane was hinting that his brother's death had really been a suicide, not an accident, that Shane had been letting me know he was still angry and upset that his brother would desert him on purpose.

When Rhett died, I remembered, the King family'd had a big hassle collecting on the youth's life insurance, so there must have been a question about whether he'd died by suicide or by accident. The policy hadn't been in effect long enough to cover death by suicide. But if Rhett's fatal overdose was accidental, the insurance company had to pay the beneficiaries. In the end, the Kings had to threaten to sue before their check was forthcoming.

As I listened to the tape, I wondered whether, like his brother, Shane King had had a life insurance policy and, if he did, who his beneficiary was.

Making notes as the taped interview wound to an end, I heard Shane telling me about his girlfriend, whose name was Tiffany Novotny. She was twenty years old, a runner-up in the Miss California contest, and an aspiring actress. I remembered Shane's showing me her photograph—a theatrically lighted head-and-shoulders shot of an extremely pretty young woman with a mass of curly dark hair and big gray eyes. In another photo in a gold frame on Shane's desktop, the same model-thin young woman had posed in a one-piece bathing suit with a banner worn diagonally across her chest identifying her as "Miss Palms."

Shane had told me that Tiffany lived with some relatives in the Palms section of Los Angeles, not at his place in Malibu. But, from the lovesick way he'd talked about her, I figured he had plans to change that as soon as possible. Now it was too late.

I located Tiffany Novotny's phone number by calling the Screen Actors Guild's agency roster, which gave me the name of her agent. He put me onto her publicist, who sounded thrilled at the prospect that the *Hollywood Star* might actually want to interview Tiffany. He obviously knew nothing about her boyfriend's being found dead that morning and I didn't enlighten him. Tiffany was a raw beginner in the industry, with little more than a few bit parts and a minor beauty pageant title to her name. She was not the type of client for whom it's easy to get publicity, either good or bad. If I did the kind of story on Tiffany that her flack was envisioning, he would probably take credit for placing it and quickly increase the monthly fee he charged her.

I dialed the number the publicist gave me, but reached only the young woman's phone machine. I left a message for her to call me either here at the *Star* or at home.

Before I left the office, I copied what I'd written for Shane King's obituary onto a floppy disk and put it into my purse. If Tiffany called me at home tonight, I wanted to be able to add her information to my notes, maybe finish some more of my story before returning to the office tomorrow.

"Don't forget you've got that screening tonight," Lucy reminded me as I got ready to leave.

My mind went blank. "Screening?"

"The new Oliver Stone film, don't you remember?" Since that morning, my mind had obviously turned to mush. "Damn, I completely forgot," I admitted. With a flash of guilt, I remembered that I'd asked Uncle Teddy to accompany me to tonight's studio screening. I knew he'd been looking forward to hobnobbing with some of his old cronies there.

My uncle, Theodore Collins, known to almost everyone in the industry as Teddy, was a successful art director until a few years ago, when he retired. Now, at seventy-four, this gentle man who raised me from babyhood after my parents died still loved keeping his eye on the industry to which he'd devoted his life. Most of all, he enjoyed trading tidbits of gossip with his old friends, and tonight's event promised to replenish his supply.

I doubted that Oliver Stone would notice my absence if I didn't go, but I didn't want to let Teddy down. "Thanks, Lucy," I said with a sigh. "I'll try to make it."

My audio tape and computer disk in my purse, I headed for home.

Uncle Teddy was in his kitchen, making his favorite fresh tomato sauce for pasta when I got to his big two-story Spanish house in Pacific Palisades. Since his retirement, he's worked hard at becoming a gourmet cook, and he's been known to give some of the best small dinner parties in Hollywood.

"Ummm. Garlic," I said, breathing in the rich, pungent odor that filled the big room.

"Have to watch who we breathe on tonight," he said, stretching around to give me a quick peck on the cheek. Teddy's thin gray mustache tickled me. He was dressed in a white chef's apron over a pale blue silk shirt and tailored gray Armani slacks. No jeans and T-shirts for Uncle Teddy, even when he was relaxing at home; he was elegance personified, always had been. He'd even managed to keep his apron a pristine white. "Rough day, sweetheart?" he asked me. "You look like you've been through the wringer, pardon my saying so."

Nothing much gets past Uncle Teddy. "You might say that," I told him. "The subject of my morning interview died a few hours before I got there, and my afternoon interview cancelled on me, for the fourth time. Other than that, it's been a really great day."

Frowning at my feeble attempt at black humor, Teddy pulled the cork out of a bottle of Merlot and deftly poured a couple of inches into a crystal wine goblet. "Here, darling, drink up, it'll make you feel better." Obediently, I took the glass and sipped, holding the dry, musty wine on my tongue for a moment before swallowing. "Want to talk about it?" Teddy picked up a scissors and began snipping bits of fresh basil into the large blue-flowered china bowl that held the chopped tomatoes and minced garlic.

Kicking off my shoes, I perched on one of the kitchen stools Teddy kept next to his kitchen counter. My long legs wouldn't fit under the tiled counter, so I sprawled sideways. "Shit, Teddy," I said, "I was supposed to interview Peter King's boy, Shane, this morning. You remember the Kings, don't you?" He nodded. "I just don't get it," I said. "Shane was only twenty-three years old, he had a great job, he was being paid a goddamned fortune. What the hell did he need to go and screw around with drugs for?" Relieved to be able to unburden myself to someone I trusted implicitly, I told my uncle all about Shane King's overdose and my conversation with Detective Tracy Lewis. The more I talked, the more I began to shake. By the time I finished with my tale, Teddy had his arms around me and my face was buried against his thin chest.

"You actually found the boy. Jesus, Quinn, that's rough." He gently stroked my hair the way he used to do when I was a child and I'd been upset about something. I still found it comforting.

I lifted my face. "Oh, damn, now look what I've done." The front of Teddy's once-white apron was streaked brown with my mascara.

Teddy lifted my chin with a finger. "It's only an apron, Quinn honey. You've got to get some perspective here."

He was right. Here a young man was dead and I was worrying about a dirty apron. My mind felt so muddled I couldn't think straight.

"This is Peter King's younger boy, right?" Teddy asked. At seventy-four, he often has far better recall than I do, especially for tidbits about Hollywood people.

"Right." I could hear the wistful quality in my own voice.

"Handsome man, that Peter King. There was a youthful Cary Grant quality about him when he was younger. Still interested, Quinn?"

"In Peter?" I should have known that Teddy would remember my affair. He probably had my entire love life chronicled somewhere in that vast storage area he called his memory. "Of course I'm not still interested," I said quickly. But I wondered whether that was really true. "It was okay while it lasted, though." I could feel myself blushing as I recalled some of the evenings Peter King and I had spent together all those years ago. I've had my share of lovers since then, of course, but there was something about Peter that was hard to duplicate. I'd even been willing to overlook all the manure his ex-wife kept shoveling in our direction. For a time, anyway. Our affair always had problems, but at least it was never dull.

For a fleeting moment, my thoughts leapt back to one particularly memorable night toward the end. It involved some warm oils and a massage technique Peter had learned in the Far East.

Teddy brought me back to reality. "The man's not marriage material," he warned. "He's a three-time loser, or maybe it's four—who can keep track these days?"

"You keep forgetting, Teddy, I'm not looking for marriage material. Quinn Collins, career woman, is not the marrying kind."

I wasn't being defensive; I meant what I said. Growing up in Hollywood, I couldn't recall seeing even one solid, lasting marriage in my social circle. I had no role models, no incentive to seek marriage as a personal goal. Everyone I knew had been divorced at least once, if not two or three times, usually messily. Sylvia St. Clair, who was Teddy's best friend and our next-door neighbor had been divorced four times and widowed once. Now somewhere in her mid-to-late seventies, Sylvia lived alone in a somewhat damp old mansion and called upon Teddy to be her escort whenever she needed one. "I've got the perfect arrangement right here," she often told me. "A handsome, debonair escort on call, and I don't have to put up with some old fart snoring in my ear every night."

The truth is, the only really stable, committed love relationship I ever witnessed close up was the one my uncle had with his longtime companion, Arthur Bates. Teddy and

Artie were a mutually adoring couple for more than thirty years and, as far as I know or ever want to know, they were completely faithful to each other right up until Artie's death three years ago. Their relationship hardly qualified as a traditional marriage, however. Even in supposedly liberal Hollywood, they kept their union mainly in the closet. For appearance's sake, Artie lived in the guesthouse that's now my home, and only their most trusted friends knew them as a couple.

At forty-three, I was definitely not sorry I'd never taken the marriage plunge. I thought of my chosen single status as a sensible method of self-preservation in the crazy world I lived in, a world I truly loved and had no intention of ever leaving—not willingly, anyway. There was probably no place else I could ever fit in. I also wasn't sorry that I'd never brought children into my strange world, where chances are they'd have grown up warped in some important way. No, I didn't need marriage or children, but that didn't mean I couldn't enjoy a fling now and then. I had nothing against either men or sex, as long as they didn't try to take over the very nice life I'd created for myself.

"Your life, your choice, darling," Teddy said as he went back to his cooking. He splashed olive oil generously into his bowl and mixed it into his aromatic concoction. "But a word to the wise. If I were a superstitious man, I might think your friend Peter King was jinxed. Be careful, it might rub off on you."

I knew what he meant. Peter's three marriages had all bitten the dust, both of his sons were now dead of drug overdoses or maybe suicide, and his movie career had hit the skids. What next? Still, the man had an incredibly sexy way of—But, enough of that.

"There was something else about those King youngsters," Teddy said, resting his mixing spoon on a large, clean scallop shell and covering the china bowl with a matching plate.

"What?"

"Can't put my finger on it right now. A scandal of some kind, I think, a death, maybe . . ." He pulled on a corner of his mustache and thought hard for a moment. "I think it was the older boy who was involved somehow, something to do with a girl. Isn't it always? But—Well, it'll come back to me." He filled a Dutch oven with water, added a dash of salt, and set it on his new stainless steel, restaurant-size stove, then gestured toward his bowl of pasta sauce. "I certainly hope you're going to help me eat this before we leave for our screening."

I suddenly realized I was starving. The morning's shock must have been wearing off. "If you don't stop cooking like this, Teddy," I warned, "I'm going to turn into a fat old broad."

"Don't talk like that, Quinn! You're not fat, you're statuesque. And I cook only healthy food. Olive oil, fresh tomatoes, a little Parmesan—nothing there to make you fat. Or old."

"Right," I said, patting my left hip.

In any other world, Teddy's assessment would be correct. I'm five feet ten and I weigh just under a hundred and fifty pounds—well within the boundaries of a normal height-to-weight distribution. When I'd tried for a career in movie acting some years back, however, I was constantly being told I was too big, too busty, too zoftig for the screen. I naturally have curves, probably more than my share, and the camera hasn't loved curves since the fifties. A really tall woman like me has to have Geena Davis's willowy figure to make it in this business, while my shape has always been much more like Marilyn Monroe's, only longer. All I can say is that Marilyn was lucky she was hot nearly a half-century ago. By today's show biz standards, she'd be considered downright fat.

"Six o'clock," Teddy told me. "Syl's coming, too, just for dinner. Why don't you go get cleaned up, sweetheart? Change your clothes, comb your hair, fix your makeup. You'll knock 'em dead tonight, make your old uncle proud. You'll feel better, trust me."

Teddy looked so eager for an evening out among industry people that I didn't have the heart to say I'd rather stay home and wait for a phone call from Tiffany Novotny, a phone call that might never come. And maybe he was right; I needed some cheering up.

So I nodded my agreement and made my way out the kitchen door and across the pool decking to my own small corner of the world.

I spent the next morning working at home. My little guesthouse has a bedroom, a living room that overlooks the pool area, and a compact kitchen. It also has a separate small dining room that I've converted into my home office. Whenever I eat at home, I do it at a two-seater table in a corner of my kitchen, so I don't really need the dining room for its intended purpose. I have a desk, a computer table, a swivel chair, and a narrow, floor-to-ceiling bookcase in my cozy workspace. It's a quiet, comfortable place for me to write, and I'm never more than a step or two away from the coffee pot.

After my morning swim and my shower, I poured my first cup of coffee for the day and phoned Detective Tracy Lewis. He told me that the autopsy on Shane King had found that the young man died of a heart attack, most likely brought on by an overdose of heroin. It would be several more days before toxicological reports officially confirmed that heroin was indeed found in Shane's organs, but the syringe found near his body had contained traces of the drug.

"I'd be surprised as hell if it turned out to be anything other than heroin," the detective told me. "With this real pure stuff we're seeing lately, sometimes we find 'em dead with the needle still sticking in their arm."

Trying not to dwell upon the gruesome image Lewis had just implanted in my mind, I told him that I would use the words "suspected drug overdose" in my obituary notice. When the lab report confirmed what he and the coroner suspected, I would follow up with a second story in the *Hollywood Star.*

After talking to Tracy, I turned on my computer, called up my unfinished obituary notice, and added the purported cause of Shane's death. I got the rest of the information I needed from the Brentwood funeral home where the young man's body had been sent after the autopsy. The funeral director told me that Shane's mother, Veronica Meyers, had another son, aged twelve, and a daughter, aged ten, by her second husband, Vito Morelli. I added the children's names to Shane's list of survivors. The funeral service was scheduled for the next morning, well before the next issue of the *Star* would hit the newsstands, so I left out that information. After rereading what I'd written, I made a few minor changes in the wording, then printed out my story and faxed it over to the office. I still prefer to use the fax machine instead of e-mail whenever possible. It seems so much safer, more secure, somehow. Or maybe I'm just old-fashioned.

As the last page of the obit exited the fax machine, the telephone rang.

"Quinn Collins," I answered.

"Uh, hi," a shaky female voice said. "Uh, this is Tiffany Novotny. My, uh, my publicist said you wanted to talk to me?"

"Oh, yes. Hello, Ms. Novotny." My mind spun wildly for a moment as I tried to decide how to approach Shane's girlfriend. I opted for the truth. "First, I want to tell you how sorry I am about your friend, Shane King," I told her. "I know you two were very close."

"Yeah, but—Hey, is this about Shane? I thought—" Her voice trailed off.

I told Shane King's girlfriend about my young moguls story, leaving out my opinion that he had been by far the least talented member of the group. "I'd already interviewed Shane once at his office, Ms. Novotny, and we had a second appointment scheduled for his home in Malibu yesterday morning. But, when I got to Shane's house—Well, unfortunately, he was already dead."

"Ohmygod, are you the one—Are you the one who—who, like, *found* him?"

"Yes, yes I am."

"Oh." I thought I detected a sniffling sound coming over the phone line, but I couldn't be sure. It could have been static. One part of my job that I absolutely loathe is having to approach the bereaved soon after they've lost a loved one. Luckily, as a show business reporter, I don't have to do that very often. My beat seldom includes the often fatal events that mainstream reporters routinely write about—plane crashes, automobile accidents, suicides, war, serial killings.

"I honestly am very sorry about Shane, Tiffany. May I call you Tiffany?"

She sniffed once more. "Yeah, sure."

"I'd like to talk to you about Shane as soon as possible. With your help, I think I can still make something of my story."

"I don't think I can tell you anything important about Shane, really I don't." Tiffany Novotny was sounding more decisive now. I wondered whether any other reporters had tried to contact her. I guessed not. Shane King hadn't really been that important in the industry yet, and I doubted that many of my ranks knew about his involvement with the former Miss Palms anyway.

"Why don't you let me be the judge of that, Tiffany? All I'm asking you to do is talk to me for a little while. Who knows, it might even make you feel better to talk to somebody else who knew Shane." Yeah, right, I thought. And it might snow in Beverly Hills tomorrow, too. As I heard the con job that was coming out of my mouth, I couldn't help feeling a little sleazy.

"I dunno. My publicist said you wanted to do a story about me, that a story in the *Hollywood Star* would help my career. But, uh, if this is just about me and Shane, I dunno—"

"Wait a minute, Tiffany." So that's it, I thought. The young woman's reluctance to talk to me wasn't so much that she was broken up about her boyfriend as that she wanted to be sure she'd get some good publicity for herself. There's no business like show business. "Maybe I didn't put it well," I told her. "This would mean publicity for you. After all, you're one of Shane's survivors, right? You were important to him, extremely important, from what he told me. My story will give the *Hollywood Star*'s readers a chance to become acquainted with you. Your name will be in it prominently, and we might even run your picture. Shane showed me a particularly attractive photograph of you he had in his office at Calistoga."

"My Miss Palms picture?"

"Yes, plus another one, a head shot. You're a very pretty young woman, Tiffany. It's not hard to see why you won that contest." Once I got started, I really piled it on thick.

"And you'd, like, definitely use my picture in the *Star*?"

"I can't promise that for sure, Tiffany. I'm not the layout editor. But I'll certainly strongly suggest we use your picture. Now, how soon can you talk with me?"

"I—I dunno. I'm having my hair done this afternoon. Shane's funeral's tomorrow morning, and I think I ought to look my best? You know, like, out of respect?" She was back to sounding unsure of herself, to ending her statements with a question mark. "Maybe some time afterward—"

This girl had very strange priorities, I thought, but who was I to judge her? I simply had a job to do. "How's right now?" I asked her. "I could be at your place in twenty minutes, twenty-five at the most. That'll give you plenty of time to get your hair done this afternoon."

"I probably ought to, like, check it out with my publicist? I mean, he thought—"

"Tiffany, my paper goes to press on Thursday. If I don't talk with you today, I'm afraid I'll have to leave you out of my story. I mean, I'm trying to be sympathetic here, to work around your schedule, but I'm on a deadline."

"Well, okay. I guess it'll be all right?" She gave me her address in Palms and I agreed to meet her there at eleven o'clock.

As I hung up the phone, I felt a little guilty, as though I was somehow helping to rob Shane King of a decent mourning period. Despite my sales pitch, I was a little disappointed that Tiffany Novotny hadn't told me to bug off. I would have liked her better if she'd been so overcome by grief that her career was the last thing on her mind. But it was obvious the only reason she'd agreed to see me was to further that career, such as it was. She probably didn't give a hoot about what I wrote about her dead boyfriend.

I felt sorry for Shane. He'd clearly misplaced his youthful affections. His purported romance with Tiffany Novotny seemed just one more thing about Shane King that didn't quite add up.

3

The house where Tiffany Novotny lived was one of those nondescript little Spanish bungalows that sprang up on palm tree-lined streets around Los Angeles after World War II. With a faded and cracked tan stucco exterior and a classic red tile roof, it sat on a forty-foot lot, squeezed in between two similar-looking neighbors. Rusting security bars guarded its windows from intruders. If the house had a garage, which I couldn't tell from the street, it had to be the old-fashioned, detached kind that was set behind the house on an alley.

Tiffany answered the door before I had a chance to ring the doorbell. Shane King's photographs didn't really do her justice; she was even prettier than I'd expected, with classic features framed by soft black curls. My guess was that she'd have been more attractive yet with a bit less goo on her face, particularly around her clear gray eyes. But moderation in anything is a rare commodity in this town. Tiffany was dressed completely in black, but her outfit—skintight black miniskirt, black stockings, snug black sweater, black lizard-skin high heels—made her look more like a cocktail waitress than someone deep in mourning. She had an eager smile on her face; as far as I could see, grief hadn't dimmed her beauty a bit.

She led me into the small living room, where she perched on the edge of a faded rose-colored velvet chair and I sank down into an overstuffed gray sofa. The furniture in this room was sixties-style stuff—never really elegant in its day, now it was shabby and worn. The walls were decorated with prints of idyllic landscapes by Constable and his contemporaries—cool scenes of a British countryside completely unlike this street with its smog-damaged palm trees and brown-patched lawns. The brightest spots of color in the room were strategically placed framed photographs of Tiffany. My guess was that the relatives with whom this young woman lived had no children of their own to display.

With an uncertain smile, Tiffany picked a fat book bound in pink imitation leather off the scratched walnut coffee table and handed it to me. "I thought you might want to, like, see my scrapbook to start," she said. "I was Miss Salinas before I moved down here, you know. And I had the lead in my high school play senior year. Maria in 'West Side Story.' The local newspaper said I was awesome, even better than Natalie Wood in the movie."

I looked through the scrapbook for a minute or two, just long enough to avoid being rude. "Any professional experience, Tiffany?" I asked, taking my notebook out of the oversize tan leather shoulder bag I always carry.

"Well, uh, yeah, extra work, stuff like that? And I had three whole lines on 'Baywatch.' I've, like, only been here in L.A. for six months and it's sorta hard to get noticed, you know?" She pulled at the hem of her skirt. "Shane was gonna help me get movie parts, told me he had something lined up for me at Calistoga—you know, the studio where he worked? I was gonna be either the ingenue or the hero's sister, it wasn't decided yet, in this comedy with Billy Crystal or Tom Hanks or somebody big like that. But now—"

"Now your getting a role in a Calistoga picture's not quite so certain, huh?"

For the first time, Tiffany's pretty face registered something resembling sadness. "Well, maybe I can still get one of the parts. But, you know—connections help?"

No lie. Particularly for young women whose major—or possibly their only—talent was their looks. Maybe it wasn't fair for me to judge Tiffany Novotny solely on my first impression of her, but I couldn't help thinking this girl was not going to be the next Meryl Streep. My guess was, if she got really lucky, she might be the next Anna Nicole Smith.

I led Tiffany through a short Q and A session, during which she offered me a selection of fascinating facts about herself, such as that she lived here in Palms with her Aunt Emma and Uncle Ralph, both of whom worked for Albertson's supermarket chain and were "totally, a thousand percent" dedicated to helping her become a movie star. They just knew she could do it, and they'd lived here in L.A. for thirty years, so of course they knew show business inside out. Also that Tiffany had been the apple of her father's eye. Apparently good old dad, who was a strawberry farmer outside Salinas, had told Tiffany she was much prettier than Julia Roberts, and far more talented, too. Needless to say, she believed him wholeheartedly.

Maybe somebody's readers couldn't wait to read juicy tidbits like these, but they sure weren't mine. I made a few notes, knowing I would undoubtedly throw them away as soon as I got back to the office.

When I felt I'd put enough time in on my bogus fluff piece about Tiffany Novotny, budding actress, I steered the conversation around to Shane King.

"Shane was cool," Tiffany told me, recrossing her shapely legs. A run was starting in her right stocking. "I mean, he was, like, totally good to me. You know, like, he paid off my whole VISA bill for me once when my checking account got overdrawn? And know what he gave me for my birthday? The cutest little red car you ever saw. A Miata, you know, it's Japanese? It used to be his, but then he, like, got the Jag? And, like I said, Shane was totally gonna help me with my career."

"Did Shane ever talk to you about his job with Calistoga Pictures?" I asked, surreptitiously glancing at my watch. Tiffany's hair appointment was in less than an hour. I had to get cracking if this interview was going to be worth anything at all.

"Not much. 'Cept for how he could get me parts in their movies." One of Tiffany's manicured hands crept toward her hair and she began to twist a curl around her finger. To my eye, she didn't look like she needed a trip to the hairdresser's, but then what did I know? I've never been particularly obsessed with my looks. At least not that obsessed. Well, not since I was twelve or thirteen, anyway. "Shane was sure I was going to be a big star, just like my dad said," Tiffany added. "I mean, he said I, like, had the looks for it?" She waited for me to indicate that I agreed with Shane's opinion before she continued. I played along, nodding slightly. "And Shane had awesome connections in the industry. He said we couldn't lose if we stuck together. We'd be like, you know, maybe Julie Andrews and Blake Edwards? Or maybe Marsha Mason and Neil—, uh, Neil Whatever?"

"Neil Simon."

"Right, that's the guy."

Despite her professed acting ambitions, Tiffany didn't appear to be the least bit embarrassed that she didn't know the name of one of America's foremost modern playwrights, even though she'd easily recalled the name of the actress he'd once been married to.

" 'Cept, of course," she went on, "Shane and me, we're

way younger than those guys."

I had to give her credit—this young woman could turn any subject into a promotion of herself, her physical appearance, and her supposedly pending stardom in a flash. "Do you know what exactly Shane did at Calistoga Pictures?" I asked her.

Spotting the run in her stocking, Tiffany casually draped a hand over it, hiding it from view. "He was, like, in charge of movies for TV, I think. Or he was gonna be, after he got trained and all."

"Seems like an awfully important job for somebody so young."

"Like I said, you gotta have connections in this town. Shane knew the right people, so he got the job, okay? I think some big shot at Calistoga was, like, a friend of his family or something."

Tiffany was probably right, I thought. I certainly hadn't uncovered any evidence that Shane had been hired for any reason other than his connections. "I guess Shane must have been under a lot of pressure at Calistoga," I suggested. "It must have been hard for him, trying to handle a big job like that when he was so young. I'll bet he got really nervous about letting his friends down."

"Shane? Oh, no, he wasn't ever freaked out about his job. Not that he ever told me, anyway."

Then maybe he didn't tell his girlfriend everything, I thought; Shane had to have some reason to be using drugs. Or maybe my thinking was old-fashioned; a lot of people probably used drugs for no better reason than because they were available. "I understand you and Shane were pretty close," I said to Tiffany. She nodded. "He mentioned something about you two planning to live together at his place in Malibu." I was trying to maneuver myself closer to the more personal aspects of their relationship, to belly up to the drug question.

"Yeah, well, he wanted me to move in with him, sure," she said, chewing on her blood-red lower lip. "But I told him I didn't know yet. I mean, I couldn't afford to—uh, I guess I didn't really want to limit myself, you know?"

"You mean to one man?"

Tiffany squirmed a bit on the rose-colored chair, for the first time looking a little bit uncomfortable. "It's just that—well, I'm only twenty, you know? And, it's awesome—I have my whole career, my whole life to think about."

"And you didn't know whether Shane King would really turn out to be another Blake Edwards. Or Neil Simon." My sympathy for poor dead Shane was growing.

She began to pick at the run in her stocking. "It's just that, I mean, I'm not, like, ready to get married or anything. And Shane—"

"Shane wanted to get married?" Maybe the red Miata had been an engagement present as well as a birthday gift.

"I dunno—not really, I guess. I think he wanted to, like, sort of own me, to keep me away from other guys. Sometimes he acted way jealous of me, know what I mean?" Tiffany stared at her feet in their ridiculously high-heeled shoes; she was obviously uncomfortable now.

I wondered whether Shane had experimented with heroin to ease the pain of Tiffany's turning him down. Whatever his reason, my time was running short and I felt I was getting nowhere fast with this interview. I had not learned one printable detail in the entire time I'd been talking to young Tiffany Novotny. It was time to cut to the chase. "How often did Shane use drugs?" I asked her, my gaze locking onto her flawless face. The only reaction I detected there was slight surprise.

"Drugs? Whaddya mean drugs? Like aspirin or penicillin or something?"

"Not quite. Like grass, coke, heroin, whatever. Illegal drugs."

"Not Shane." She shook her head firmly. "Shane was, like, way freaked out when it came to drugs. You know, like he was too chicken to even try anything?" I got the impression that Tiffany wouldn't have minded trying something herself. "I guess 'cause of what happened to his brother," she said. "I mean, even when we made the club scene, like we'd go to Shadow's every once in a while? Shane would just stand there, sort of staring at people with this look on his face. You know, like he was better than everybody else 'cause he didn't use and they all did? I mean, maybe he drank a little beer or wine once in a while, one or two glasses at the most. But Shane was never a *user.*"

"Never?"

"Nope."

What Tiffany described jibed with what Shane had told me, but it certainly didn't explain that empty syringe found near his Jacuzzi, or how he had ingested whatever it was that had killed him. "So, if he didn't use drugs, how do you think he died?" I asked her.

Tiffany shrugged her shoulders. "I heard he had a heart attack while he was in his hot tub. Isn't that right?"

I sighed. "Tiffany, twenty-three-year-old men don't generally have fatal heart attacks—in or out of hot water—unless they have a congenital defect or a rare disease or something." Her gray eyes were blank, uncomprehending. "The cops found a used hypodermic syringe lying on the floor tiles next to Shane's Jacuzzi," I told her.

"Ohmygod—you mean like a needle?" There was sheer repulsion in her voice.

"Right, the kind they give shots with." Tiffany cringed visibly and began to chew on one of her long red thumbnails. "This particular syringe had heroin residue in it, Tiffany," I told her. Now, despite her heavy makeup and provocative clothing, Tiffany Novotny looked more like a child playing dress-up than a beauty queen or aspiring movie star. "It'll take a while for the final autopsy results to come back," I added, "but the cops're pretty sure Shane's heart attack was caused by an overdose of heroin."

"But how—?" Her face crumbled. "I mean, shit, Shane didn't hardly even drink wine except on real special occasions. I mean, he could be an awesome pain in the butt about it sometimes. You know, everybody at least smokes a little grass once in a while, just to fit in or make sex bet—I don't mean needles or anything—no hardcore stuff." She shuddered and made a sour face. "But no, uh uh, not Shane." She shook her head determinedly, making her springy curls bounce. "I'm sorry, Ms. Collins, but you gotta be dead wrong about this."

"Maybe," I conceded. "Like I said, the test results haven't come back yet." Maybe Shane did have some kind of congenital heart defect after all, I began to think. Or maybe the thermostat on his hot tub had malfunctioned and the thing had literally boiled him to death. But, if so, what was that syringe doing in his bedroom? And why hadn't the initial autopsy discovered either something wrong with his heart or physical evidence of his body overheating?

"This club scene you describe," I said, "I'd like to know more about that. Might be another story there." An idea was beginning to creep into my head—a feature on drug usage in Hollywood. I could include quotes about the users who'd OD'd and died, like John Belushi and River Phoenix, along with interviews with the ones who'd gone the Betty

Ford Clinic route. They frequently turned into missionaries for the recovery process and were anxious to talk to the press about overcoming their habits. Then there was always Robert Downey, Jr.'s collection of drug troubles. I already had a thick file on him. I figured I could use Shane's death in the lead of my story, include it as my reason for writing this kind of analytical article now.

The more I thought about it, the more I felt it would work. Despite all the press coverage claiming it was an aberration every time somebody big bit the dust as a result of addiction, everybody in Hollywood knew that drug use and abuse was still rampant in the industry. I wondered how much money cocaine, speed, grass, heroin, whatever, cost the movie business each year. Not just the money spent directly on the drugs themselves, but in terms of lost production time on sets, unshootable scripts delivered weeks past deadline, actors and directors whose chemical habits robbed them of their youth and talent. And why did drug usage seem to be so much more prevalent in show biz than in other industries? At first blush, it seemed a very promising story concept.

"I—I don't really know anything much about the club scene," Tiffany told me. "Like I said, Shane and I didn't hang around them much. It's, like, *boring* when you're the only one there who's sober." She had a wistful look on her face, as though she'd missed a great opportunity. I wondered whether she was thinking about Shane, or lost chances to get high.

"When you went to the clubs, where exactly did you go?"

"Well, there's the Viper Room and the Green Room, places like that. Or Whiskey a Go Go. But the really awesome ones, they change their locations all the time, you know? I mean, they rent an old warehouse or something for a few weeks, then pack up and move when the cops start coming around. I mean, like, nobody wants to risk getting arrested or anything, right?"

"So how's anybody supposed to know where that kind of party is going to be on a given evening?"

Tiffany shrugged her shoulders and avoided making eye contact with me. "I dunno," she said. "People just tell you, that's all."

"You mean your friends?"

"Yeah, like that. Or just somebody you meet someplace." Fidgety now, she made a point of glancing at her watch, then picked up the pink scrapbook. "You gonna need to borrow this or anything?"

"Huh? Oh, no, I think I looked through it pretty thoroughly already."

"What about my picture, then? You gonna send over a photographer or do you want me to give you one of my composites?"

"The composite would be best, I think, Tiffany. In view of my deadline and all."

Tiffany got up and walked toward the back of the house. She took small steps, keeping her spine ramrod-straight, as though she had a stack of books balanced on her head. Obviously, this girl had taken modeling lessons. Or maybe her walk was just the residue of all those beauty contests she'd been in. I put my notebook back into my purse. My time here was up and I really couldn't say I was sorry. Tiffany clearly didn't want to talk about the Hollywood drug scene, assuming she knew much of anything about it. And we seemed to have exhausted her meager knowledge of Shane King's unexpected death.

"Thanks," I said, when Tiffany returned with her composite—an eight-by-ten color glossy that showed four shots of her pretty face bordering a larger one of her posing in a bathing suit. Unlike many actresses' composites, Tiffany's head-and-shoulders poses were all pretty much alike—smiling, sexy, dramatically sober, but always showing nothing more than a beautiful young brunette exploiting her good looks.

Most I've seen over the years—those chosen by more serious thespians—featured their subjects trying to look as different as possible in each shot. One pose might show an attractive young mom opening a can of soup while the one next to it featured the same actress dressed as an Eastern European peasant or a stripper. But then, maybe Tiffany Novotny aspired to only one type of role.

I slid the composite into the side pocket of my purse. "I'll pass this on to the layout artist as soon as I get back to the office," I told her, "and thanks for talking to me."

Tiffany walked me to the door. "So when's this gonna be in the *Star*?" she asked.

"I'll try my best to get something into this week's edition," I said, feeling vaguely guilty. I knew there was little information here that I could use. I handed her one of my cards. "If you think of anything else I should know about Shane, give me a call, will you?"

"Uh, sure, I guess." Her face fell.

"And let me know if you get that part in the Calistoga movie, okay?"

The smile was back. "Hey, yeah, sure, I'll do that."

"So probably I'll see you tomorrow," I told her.

"Tomorrow?"

"At Shane's funeral."

"Oh, right." That her lover's impending memorial service had momentarily slipped her mind didn't seem to embarrass Tiffany Novotny in the least.

As I drove back toward the office, I couldn't help but wonder what the King family had thought about young Shane's choice in women. But then, with each of his parents married three times, mainly miserably, they'd hardly been in a position to criticize their young son's folly.

"Quinn, for godsake, do I have to remind you again that advertisers keep the *Star*'s doors open? Or just exactly who our advertisers are?" My partner and co-publisher, Harry Radner had an exasperated look on his face and his voice dripped with sarcasm. Waving his hands in the air like a couple of loose canaries as he paced my office, he didn't really expect an answer to his question. We'd had this kind of discussion many times before.

"It'll be a good story, Harry, and you know it." I had returned to the office in Santa Monica and was attempting to lunch on a takeout salad at my desk when Harry came in. I'd made the mistake of telling him about my latest stroke of journalistic genius. Now I leaned back in my desk chair and watched as he took four long strides in one direction, then four in the other. My office is not large. I could probably pace it in three strides. Harry's all of five feet five and he probably doesn't weigh a hundred and twenty-five fully dressed. He also has a tendency to make me feel physically mammoth, so I usually remain seated whenever I'm around him.

"Sure, Ms. Woodward-and-Bernstein. And Universal and Twentieth are gonna buy up all our extra copies, pass 'em out to their stockholders at annual meetings. What do you think we are, the fucking *L.A. Times*?" Harry's hands flew upward again. He's nothing if not hyper. Harry Radner's always had enough energy for five people twice his size.

As I could have predicted, Harry didn't exactly share my enthusiasm for my proposed article about drug use in the industry the *Hollywood Star* covered. His argument was that our advertisers all came from that same industry. So, if we wrote something that was perceived as trashing show business, we stood to lose our advertisers. And, without advertisers, we'd quickly go broke. I had to admit he had a point. Still, I liked to consider myself a journalist, not a pimp for Hollywood.

"Don't we have a duty to those stockholders to tell them the truth about how their investments are being used, Harry?" I argued, pushing around a piece of romaine with my plastic fork. I caught our secretary, Lucy, watching the little scene in my office with interest, a by-product of having an office door that hadn't closed right since the big quake. She rolled her eyes.

"Our principle duty is to stay in business, Quinn. You know—" Harry rubbed two fingers against his thumb and waved them under my nose. "—sometimes I think you just don't understand the basic concept of capitalism. You think we pay the printer's bills and buy paper and make the rent on this palatial suite of offices, plus give you a decent return on your investment with some kind of magic?"

"But if we don't print something different than what *Variety* and the *Reporter* already have, Harry, we won't be in business much longer, anyway. Way I look at it, we might as well hang onto our ethics."

"And your idea of 'something different' is a piece that says Hollywood's being run by coke heads and speed freaks? Jesus H. Christ, woman, get with the program!"

Now it was my turn to be exasperated. "Let me say it one more time, partner. My idea is simply to find out whether or not Hollywood has a collective drug problem that's adversely affecting its corporate balance sheets. I'm not out to do a personal smear job on anybody." I held up both hands in a gesture of peacemaking. "I'm simply seeking the truth."

Harry threw himself into a chair and exhaled loudly, playing the part of somebody who'd exhausted his last scrap of energy with this latest tirade. Like me, Harry's a failed actor. He tends toward melodrama. "Save me from the idealists. There's just no reasoning with you sometimes, Quinn. I swear . . ."

Ever since I bought a piece of the *Star*, Harry's volatility has shot into the stratosphere whenever I suggest doing an article he thinks might hurt our advertising revenues. It's as though he thinks if he just screams at me a little louder or hams it up a little more, he'll make his point that much more forcefully and I'll change my mind. The difference between now and the days before I became a partner is that before he could just say no. Now I can do whatever I damn well please.

"I'll keep your concerns in mind, Harry, the way I always do," I told him. "If you don't like my story when I've finished it, we'll talk again."

"Damn right, we'll talk again," he said, pushing himself back to his feet. As he stalked out of my office, his small shoulders slumping in his eight-hundred-dollar Italian suit, he was the picture of affluent dejection.

"Besides," I said to his retreating back, "maybe I'll find out that Hollywood doesn't even have a drug problem. Maybe Universal and Twentieth will love my story."

"Yeah. And maybe Schwartzenegger's gonna wear a dress and sing 'Dixie' in his next movie," he mumbled as he passed Lucy's desk in the reception area.

She and I exchanged grins and winks. I shoved a forkful

of salad into my mouth, then turned to my computer and typed a few notes to myself—ideas about how I could begin exploring Hollywood's current addictions.

I stayed up late that night, writing the last of my articles for the *Hollywood Star*'s next edition and faxing them to the office. Then I set my clock radio for seven. I didn't want to risk being late for Shane King's funeral. As a reporter, I didn't have to go. But as the woman who'd found Shane's body, and as a former lover of the dead youth's father, I felt a solemn obligation to be there.

I was exhausted and bleary-eyed when the seven o'clock news on KABC blasted me awake. After a moment's procrastination, I forced my eyelids open, rolled out of bed, and grabbed my bathing suit.

With the pool right outside the door of my cozy guesthouse, I figured I had no excuse not to stay in shape. Lucky for me, swimming had always been my exercise of choice; it's easy on the joints and it stretches most of the body's muscles. The only drawback was that each morning it became just a little bit harder to force myself to plunge into those cold, wet depths. Once I was in and had done a few vigorous laps, I was fine; it was just getting from my warm bed to that point that I always dreaded.

Forty laps and fifty minutes later, I'd finished my swim and was stepping out of the shower. I turned on the blow dryer and began to dry and style my hair.

I'd been keeping my dark blond hair short and simple, in deference to my daily swims. I have to confess that my hair has always been the one thing I'm rather vain about. Over the years, I'd been a flaxen blonde, a strawberry blonde, a redhead, a brownette, even a true brunette. I'd worn my locks in every style from short and curly to long and straight. I grew up in show business, remember, learning by observation that there was nothing about me (or anyone else, for that matter) that the makeup artist and the hairdresser couldn't magically improve.

Mainly, it had been fun trying on all those new looks, almost as though I could become a new person with each change. Frequently my switches coincided with the end of a romance. I'd often wondered what Freud, or even Joyce Brothers, might say about that.

Usually, I kept a new look for a year or so, until I got tired of it. That's about as long as any of my romances has lasted, too, come to think of it. My black-haired stage lasted only about two weeks, though, during which my friends treated me with a great deal of sympathy and kept offering to help me to a chair. The sharp contrast between my naturally light complexion and my new raven locks made me look so pale I appeared to be suffering from some dread disease. During those two weeks, I didn't meet one new man, either. I took that as a major clue and reverted to a lighter shade.

A few years ago, I decided to give up my frequent hairstyle changes and stick with my current color, which was a flattering two or three shades lighter than my mousy natural hue. "Honey blond" was light enough to be officially blond, but dark enough that the inevitable green tint my hair acquired from a daily dunking in a chlorinated swimming pool didn't show. So I decided to remain a honey blonde. At least until I found something I liked better.

For some reason, my love life during those years had been considerably tamer than previously, too. Maybe that was a by-product of passing forty and looking my age. Hmmm, I thought as I peered into the bathroom mirror, quickly applying my makeup. Maybe just a little bit of paler blond highlighting around my face wouldn't hurt at that.

I opened my closet and selected a dusty teal silk dress and a pair of low-heeled soft gray shoes for the funeral, the most subdued outfit I owned. Luckily, few people in California wore black to funerals anymore. Dark colors never looked good on me, so I simply didn't have any black clothes in my wardrobe. The teal would have to do.

As I left my guesthouse, I saw that Uncle Teddy was now using the pool, methodically churning his way from one end to the other at a slow, steady pace. I smiled and waved at him, saying a silent little prayer that thirty years from now I would be as motivated—and as physically fit—as my seemingly unsinkable septuagenarian uncle.

As I climbed into the Mercedes, its clock told me I had twenty minutes to make it to the funeral. If Pacific Coast Highway wasn't too clogged with traffic and parking at the funeral home wasn't a problem, I would be right on time.

Despite the queasy feeling I had whenever I thought about this morning's ceremony—and about seeing Peter King again after all those years—I turned the key in the ignition and headed the car out of the long driveway and onto Sunset Boulevard.

4

Services for Shane King were brief, non-denominational, and poorly attended. I'd been hoping I could blend into a large crowd, observe the proceedings, sign the guest book so the King family would know I'd paid my respects, and split. When it came down to it, I decided, my curiosity about seeing Peter King again was best satisfied from a good, safe distance.

Unfortunately, only about forty people showed up at the Brentwood funeral parlor, not a great turnout for a youth who'd had six different parents in his lifetime and was embarking on a career in the film business. His immediate family, plus all the step-moms, step-dads, and step- and half-siblings would account for a good portion of this crowd. Even if only half of his various family members attended—allowing for continuing domestic warfare that might keep some away—they represented a small crowd. That didn't leave all that many seats here being filled by people who fit into the categories of friends and coworkers.

I had to assume that Shane King had not been a particularly popular young man.

I slipped into a pew toward the back of the chapel and sat by myself, hands clenched in my lap, breathing in the pungent odor of the dozens of lilies that flanked the large wooden coffin at the front of the room. I was grateful the coffin was closed. I'd already seen Shane King's dead body once; I didn't particularly want to view it again, even from a distance.

I recognized few of the people in attendance. There was Peter, of course, who walked in alone and didn't appear to spot me. He stopped and exchanged handshakes and hugs with a few of the funeral-goers who'd taken aisle seats. I could see his face as he bent down to kiss the cheek of an elderly woman in a charcoal linen suit, and my heart felt a strong wrench. My former lover was almost gaunt now, and his complexion was almost as gray as the prominent streaks in his hair. Although he was only in his mid-fifties, today Peter King looked at least a decade older, a beaten man. He took a seat by himself in the front row, on the left side of the chapel.

A minute or two later, I saw Shane's mother, Veronica, being escorted by a short dark man I took to be her current husband, Joshua Meyers. Two young children, undoubtedly Veronica's offspring from her second marriage, followed close behind them. This little quartet also sat in a front pew, but they chose the one across the aisle from Peter's.

Peter and Veronica both stared straight ahead, at their younger son's coffin, careful not to look at each other. How sad, I thought, that these two couldn't give each other a crumb of solace, even on a tragic occasion like this. Surely they'd both loved Shane. He had been the only remaining product of their long-dissolved marriage. Yet there remained a visible distance—both physically and emotionally—between the two.

Among the mourners, I saw two or three minor league actors whose faces I recognized, a couple of crew members, and Parker Kellerman, Vice President of Calistoga Pictures. Parker was accompanied by a much younger man, perhaps his son, I thought, noting that both had slightly bulbous noses and heavy jaws. If the younger man had been a close friend of Shane's, maybe that accounted for the dead youth's alleged "connections" at Calistoga.

As the service was about to begin, a piece of organ music I didn't recognize rang out. I've never been into organized religion, so I'm pretty ignorant about the various melodies deemed appropriate for anything from christenings to funerals.

At the last possible moment, a young woman in a short, low-cut black ensemble and extremely high heels marched down the center aisle. I recognized the stiff-spined gait as Tiffany Novotny's and watched as she made what could be described only as a grand entrance. Cringing inwardly, I saw her reach the front pew. Her gaze darted back and forth between Peter on the left and Veronica's little group on the right. She chose to sit on Peter's side; whether that was because his pew had more available room or because of some animosity between Tiffany and her boyfriend's mother, I had no idea. She leaned over and exchanged a few words with Peter. Then the service began.

I zoned out during most of what followed, letting my glance wander randomly around the chapel, checking out what people were wearing and noting who was paying attention to the somber-faced clergyman's talk and who wasn't.

The way I figure it, when you're dead, you're dead and all the mumbo-jumbo involved in a funeral doesn't make a damn bit of difference. I don't believe in an afterlife, although I admit I could be wrong. It's just that I've never seen any evidence one exists. As a result, I've never found funerals and burial services to be particularly consoling events. Still, I certainly respect their value for other people, and I force myself to suffer through them whenever I have to.

Maybe my attitude stems from the fact that I began attending funerals when I was less than two years old, starting with my own parents'. Not that I honestly remember either my parents or their funeral, of course; I was far too young. But Uncle Teddy has told me more than once about how I cried and cried while the organist played "Amazing Grace" or some such song, completely disrupting the funeral service. In the end, he'd had to carry me out into the hallway and stuff a cookie in my mouth to get me to shut up.

My mother and father were Hollywood scriptwriters. At least they were at one time, in an earlier, happier life. My dad even got an Academy Award nomination once, for a script he'd written in the late forties. But, when the car he was driving plunged off a Malibu cliff into the sea on a rainy winter night in 1960, neither he nor my mother had worked as writers in Hollywood in more than seven years. They were both dead long before the Highway Patrol happened onto the wreck of their car the next morning.

According to Uncle Teddy, my father had once attended several meetings of an anti-fascist group that was later accused of being a Communist front organization. During the McCarthy Era, when Dad was asked to name names, he was belligerently uncooperative and, the next thing he and my mother knew, they were blacklisted. Not that my father was ever really a Communist, Teddy insists; Dad simply didn't believe it was fair to get other people into trouble in an attempt to save his own skin. Or his own livelihood. My mother's unpardonable crime was simply that she'd married my father.

Years later, of course, many of the blacklisted writers and actors in Hollywood found work again and, in many cases, they became highly admired for their resistance against the McCarthyites during Hollywood's darkest hour. By the seventies, people like Lillian Hellman were almost being deified within the industry for their earlier refusal to name names.

But, by then, my parents, Sheldon Foster and the former Megan Collins, were long dead and buried. It often pains me to know that, if he'd only lived long enough, my dad might have been considered an American hero. As it was, I knew he'd died a defeated, depressed man who couldn't even support his wife and daughter. Except for a small life insurance policy that went to me, he was nearly destitute. I think my more lasting legacy from my parents was a love of the movies and writing, the whole show business milieu. That, and perhaps a determination not to be beaten by the world that destroyed them.

Lucky for me, my mom's brother, my Uncle Teddy, was willing to take me in after my parents died. Teddy changed my last name to his and did a far better job of being both mother and father to me than I had any right to expect. Still, to this day, I truly hate funerals. They always leave me with an aching hole somewhere deep inside me.

As Shane King's funeral rites came to an end, the minister announced that the family would greet their friends in an adjoining room. Everyone began to file out toward the room indicated. My departure in another direction would have been too conspicuous, so I followed along, sheep-style, my step heavy.

Buck up, I told myself. The worst part was over. By the time I got to the reception room, I couldn't even smell the lilies.

A buffet table had been set out along one wall, offering guests a selection of salads, rolls, and sweets. I made a beeline for a cup of coffee, then balanced it in my left hand as I retreated into the crowd.

As I sipped the hot black liquid, I saw Tiffany Novotny standing and talking to Parker Kellerman and the younger man I took to be his son. Maybe there was something to be learned there, I decided, pushing my way through the crowd toward the trio.

"Tiffany," I said, nodding in her direction. She smiled and nodded in return. "And Parker, hello, nice to see you again." I thrust my free hand toward him and he shook it.

The crease between Parker Kellerman's bushy brown eyebrows deepened. "Gwen, isn't it?"

"Quinn, I corrected him. Quinn Collins, of the *Hollywood Star*."

"Right, now I remember. Quinn, this is my son, Troy."

The youth mumbled something incoherent and shot me a resentful look.

"Nice to meet you, Troy," I said. "Do you work at Calistoga, too?"

"Nope, not at present. I'm Lance Edelson's assistant right now."

I recognized the name of one of Hollywood's top agents. "Nice work if you can get it."

Troy grimaced. "Yeah, if you don't mind working your ass off."

I couldn't think of anything appropriate to say to that, so I turned back to the young man's father, who looked less than pleased with his son's ready complaint. "I'd like a few minutes of your time, Mr. Kellerman. If this isn't convenient, maybe an appointment at your office—"

"What about?"

"I've been working on a story about young executives in the industry and I'm including Shane King. You may know that I interviewed him at Calistoga last week, and I had another appointment with him this week, but—Well—I thought you might be able to fill in a few holes for me."

Kellerman looked uncomfortable for a split second, then recovered admirably. "Troy," he said, pinching the sleeve of his son's suit jacket, "why don't you and Ms. Novotny go check out the buffet table. I'll join you in a few minutes."

"Come on, Tiffany. Let's get something to eat." The grim-faced younger man's words had the distinct aura of a command, but Tiffany didn't seem to mind. Her mincing steps followed him all the way to the buffet table, where she picked a grape off of a fruit display and inserted it between her red-painted lips. Somehow, when she did it, even that small gesture seemed overtly sexual.

"So, what's on your mind, Ms. Collins?"

I kept my voice down as much as possible and hoped that the din surrounding us would be sufficient to muffle anything I had to say from the ears of eavesdroppers. "Shane seemed to be in quite a high position at Calistoga—for someone of his age and, uh, background," I said. "Were you the one who hired him?"

"I guess you could say I was instrumental in getting Shane his job, yes." Kellerman didn't elaborate.

"Mind telling me what qualified him for a position like that?"

Kellerman's gaze darted around the room a bit before he answered me. Now it was his turn to keep his voice down. "I made a mistake, all right? Shane was my son's friend—Actually, it was the older brother, Rhett, who was tight with Troy, back in high school. I was just trying to be a Good Samaritan, thought I'd give the kid a break."

Some "break," I thought, a six-figure salary and all the perks that went with it. There's nothing like starting at the top. "And now you regret having done that?" I asked.

"With the way things turned out, I—Look here, Quinn, if you want any more, it's strictly off the record."

"From here on," I agreed, reluctantly. Reporters hate to take anything off the record. Still, I'd already faxed my story about Shane and the baby moguls of Hollywood into the office. It was probably well into the production cycle by now, so my questions were mainly to satisfy my own curiosity and to provide background for my planned feature on drug abuse in the industry. "Why were you sorry you hired Shane?" I asked.

"As a production company executive, the kid was a total washout," Parker Kellerman told me, frowning. "Six feet of bad attitude, drugged up most of the time, you know the type."

I managed to keep my surprise off my face. "Are you telling me Shane came to work under the influence?" I asked.

"Hell, yes, he did, all the time. Look, I don't know what the kid was using, but he was using, all right."

"How could you tell?"

"Because he was completely erratic on the job, that's how. I'd hand him a project and a week later he wouldn't even have started it. He didn't show up for meetings. Once I even caught him asleep at his desk. His eyes always had that—that droopy look, know what I mean?" I nodded. "When I heard he'd OD'd, it was no big surprise. Not to me, it wasn't."

Out of the corner of my eye, I saw Tiffany smiling coquettishly at Troy Kellerman. Would he be her next conquest? An assistant to one of Hollywood's biggest agents and the son of a studio executive wouldn't be a bad choice at all. Still, Troy didn't look particularly smitten to me. "Did you talk to Shane about his job performance?" I asked Troy's dad.

"More than once. He'd been warned and warned again. Truth was, if he'd hauled his ass into work the day he— Well, the day he died. I—I was planning to fire him."

"That's interesting," I told him. "And Shane knew he was about to be fired?"

Kellerman pulled on his heavy chin. His beard was dark and a stubble was already beginning to appear. "If he was at all coherent, he had to know his days were numbered. But—Well, it always seems to me that druggies like him think their actions won't have consequences. Guess that crap addles their brains somehow. They sure don't think straight." He shook his head. "Hell, maybe it was something genetic with Shane. I mean, both the King kids—"

"Yeah," I said, my heart growing heavier by the minute. "Maybe it's genetic." I saw Peter King extricate himself from a group of mourners and head in our direction.

"You won't print what I said about the kid's being high at work now, right?" Kellerman's dark eyes fixed me with a stare.

"I didn't hear it from you," I said, figuring if I ever needed any of this, I'd simply use what Parker had told me to coax the same information out of some other source. So far, though, I didn't see much of anything here that I'd be likely to need.

It wasn't hard to figure out why Parker Kellerman wouldn't want to be quoted. After all, he was responsible for Shane's being on the Calistoga payroll in the first place. Obviously, hiring the youth had been a bad judgment call, and bad judgment calls frequently count against senior executives. I had no idea how Kellerman's scorecard at Calistoga looked at present, but I couldn't blame him for not wanting his latest screw-up spread all over the *Hollywood Star*.

Kellerman patted my elbow lightly in dismissal. "Better go rescue my son," he said, heading straight for the buffet table, where Tiffany was now hanging on Troy's arm.

Christ, I thought, at least the girl could have waited until Shane was actually buried before she put the make on somebody else who might help her career.

"Quinn," a familiar voice whispered in my ear as I stood frowning at the young couple.

I swiveled around, my knees quickly turning to jelly. "Hello, Peter," I said. "I can't tell you how sorry I am about Shane."

He swallowed hard. I saw that Peter King's face had new lines in it now, deep creases running down each side from cheekbones to chin, and huge, puffy bags under his eyes. The old intelligent sparkle in his gaze was gone, too, replaced by deadness. I couldn't see a trace of the "young Cary Grant quality" Uncle Teddy had commented on.

"I really need to talk to you," Peter told me.

"Uh, sure, of course, anytime."

"Not here," he said, gesturing around the room, which had begun to feel hot and claustrophobic to me. "I mean in private."

What was this about, I wondered? Certainly Peter wasn't trying to rekindle our old romance, not under these circumstances. Undoubtedly he knew I was the one who'd found his son's body. Discussing that traumatic event with the dead youth's father held no appeal for me, but I couldn't say no. Not to Peter. "Whenever—"

Peter checked his watch. I couldn't help noticing it was a Rolex. Even when this whole town knew he was on the skids, he was still trying to look like a player. I felt a surge of pity for him and his dashed hopes. "Can you make lunch?" he asked. "One o'clock, Ocean Avenue Seafood?"

"Sure. But what about the burial? Won't you have to—"

"Shane's being—" Peter's voice broke and his exhausted blue eyes grew moist. "He—he's being cremated. We're having another service—just the immediate family—next week sometime, to scatter his ashes."

"And you don't have to go back to the house or—"

"Veronica's having her people over. As usual, I'm not exactly welcome."

Was there no end to the bitterness of divorce? I reached over and squeezed Peter's hand. "One o'clock," I said.

"Thanks." He pecked me on the cheek. "You always were the best, Quinn." Then he melted back into the crowd around the buffet table.

I signed the guest book by the door and hurried outside to the parking lot, where I filled my lungs with some badly needed fresh air.

I had a spinach salad topped with warm bay scallops for lunch, along with a glass of iced tea. Peter King had half a dozen fresh oysters on the half shell. He washed them down with Ketel One on the rocks.

It was somewhere between his first and second shot of vodka that the worry lines in his face began to soften and he started to tell me what was on his mind.

"Both of them, Quinn. That's what I just can't buy. Both of them."

I reached across the table and patted Peter's hand. I couldn't think of anything appropriate to say to this man who'd lost both of his sons to drugs. We were sitting in the semi-enclosed patio area of Ocean Avenue Seafood, virtually on the sidewalk of Ocean Avenue, across the street from Palisades Park. I stared through the Plexiglas partition at a passing city bus and listened to the chirping sound of the traffic signal on the corner of Santa Monica Boulevard as it changed from WALK to WAIT. The city had installed several of the noise-making traffic lights some years ago to help the blind make their way across busy streets. "You've got to be going through hell," I said, finally, feeling inadequate.

"Rhett, maybe," Peter said. "Rhett had problems from day one, not that that makes it any easier to—I mean, Rhett got into marijuana in junior high. I didn't know about it at the time—hell, I probably didn't want to know, or maybe because of the divorce I—But he told me about it later. That was Rhett all the way—too sensitive by half, and an over-developed conscience that never let him rest." Peter pushed an ice cube around his glass with his index finger. "Know what he told me once? I think he was only about seventeen, maybe eighteen. Said he could feel his soul bleeding. *His soul bleeding!* Felt personally responsible for all the ills of the world." I nodded in sympathy. "Guess any fool would've known he'd get into stronger stuff after that girl was killed. Took it so damn hard."

"Girl?" I sat up a little straighter in my seat, recalling Uncle Teddy's foggy memory of an earlier tragedy that had somehow involved Rhett King. "What girl?"

"Classmate of Rhett's who was raped and murdered by that Mexican gang." Peter finished his third Ketel One and signaled the waiter to bring him a fourth. "Name was Lauren something, like Lauren Bacall."

The waiter took away Peter's empty glass. I declined his offer to bring me something from the bar. I figured one of us had to stay sober enough to drive Peter home, and it obviously wasn't going to be him. I knew Peter could drink hard on occasion. The signs that he'd had too much weren't always immediately evident, either. He could usually manage to hold a coherent conversation, just speaking a little slower than normal. But his motor coordination went downhill fast. Peter King had a tendency to stagger and run into things when he was drunk. As I recalled, he was no star in the bedroom under those circumstances, either. But that no longer was my concern.

"Hartley, I think her name was, or Hartman," Peter said. "Jesus, Quinn, my head feels like it's filled with cotton balls these days. Can't remember my own name sometimes." Stress and booze will do that to the best of us.

"Was Lauren a friend of Rhett's?" I asked, spearing a scallop with my fork and pushing it around my salad bowl.

"Not a close one, I don't think. They knew each other at school is all. What I'm trying to say is that Rhett always felt it was his fault she died. Right after it happened was when he started getting into the real heavy stuff—pills, coke, even heroin. Said he kept having nightmares; he was afraid to go to sleep."

"I don't get it, Peter. Why would Rhett feel responsible if some gang kids killed this Lauren girl?"

"Because he was Rhett, that's why. Like I told you, he had a way of feeling responsible for every damn thing that happened anywhere around him." Peter pushed away his plate of crushed ice and empty oyster shells. "Th—the girl was killed after a beach party she was at with a bunch of kids from Pali High. Down at Will Rogers Beach. Rhett was at the party, too, and I suppose he thought he should've kept track of her better, maybe that he should've realized she was missing earlier, something like that. How the hell do I know?" The waiter brought the fresh vodka. Peter stared at it for a moment, then took a long drink, his eyes closed as if the light suddenly was too strong. "But that wasn't my point, anyway," he said a moment later. "My point is . . ." Peter's voice trailed off and I could see his eyes losing focus.

"How about a cup of coffee, friend?" I tried to keep my

voice gentle, supportive, non-judgmental.

"Am I getting drunk?"

"A little."

"Good. Man's got two kids dead, he's got a right to get drunk."

I couldn't argue with that. Or maybe I could. "Why did you ask me here, Peter? It wasn't about Rhett, was it?"

His chin began to quiver and a small choking sound emerged from his throat. I looked away, touched and a little embarrassed. Two apparently inebriated homeless men were having an argument across the street, on the grassy strip of park land that skims the bluff above Santa Monica Beach. I watched as one shoved the other into a bulging shopping cart. He stumbled and fell to the ground. It took him a long time to get back to his feet. Then he staggered away, the dispute either settled or already forgotten.

Peter cleared his throat and wiped at his eyes with the back of his hand. "I wanted to talk to you because you—" He lowered his head and stared down at the table. "I—I just can't believe it, Quinn. Not Shane, too. Shane just wasn't fragile, not the way Rhett was. Shane was tough, I mean he could be a real son-of-a-bitch at times, if he wanted to."

"Doesn't mean he couldn't have been using drugs," I suggested.

Peter looked up at me. Some of the cloudiness began to clear from his eyes. "You don't understand, Quinn. Shane worshiped his brother, all except for the one thing. He was mad as hell at Rhett about his habit. I just can't believe he would—Not Shane."

I signaled the waiter to bring us two cups of coffee. "Shane told me the same thing when I talked with him last week," I admitted. "Said he never touched drugs because of Rhett. And Shane's girlfriend told me he almost never even had a beer or a glass of wine. But—"

"See what I mean? That's why I wanted to talk to you, Quinn. To see if there was anything that looked funny about—Well, about what you found at Shane's place."

I sipped my coffee and thought. "The house was all locked up, Peter, locked up tight. And as far as anything looking 'funny' . . . I just don't know. The other day was the only time I'd ever seen Shane's house. I don't know how it was supposed to look, and I didn't go inside. Still—You know, Peter, nobody admits using drugs if they don't have to. Isn't it possible that Shane had a secret habit? Maybe drugs were something he did all by himself, at home, when nobody was around to see. Maybe this time he simply overdid it."

"*Somebody* would have had to know about it, Quinn." Peter began to twist his crisp white napkin into a rope. "You didn't see what Rhett was like toward the end. I did. No question he was on something, or a bunch of things. Any fool could see it. He was incoherent, he was dirty, he smelled bad, his pupils were dilated, you couldn't get a straight answer out of him on any subject." I glanced quickly across the street, but the two vagrants had disappeared. "I begged him to go to AA or NA or something, to get help before—" Peter told me, "But Rhett—"

"Somebody *did* know, Peter."

His glance shot upward. "Somebody knew what?"

"At Shane's job. Somebody from Calistoga told me that Shane had been showing up for work high lately. He was about to lose his job because of it."

"I don't believe it."

I wasn't breaking my promise to Parker Kellerman, I told myself. Talking to the dead youth's anguished father about what Kellerman had told me hardly fell into the same category as publishing it in the *Hollywood Star.* I repeated our entire conversation as accurately as I could. "Why don't you talk to him yourself if you want to know more?" I suggested.

"Maybe—" Peter's jaw slackened. "But I—I just don't understand," he said, dropping his twisted napkin onto the table in front of him. "How the hell could Kellerman see it and nobody else? Tell me that."

"Maybe Kellerman wasn't the only one, Peter. Maybe lots of people at Calistoga knew. I only talked to Kellerman, remember. And, you've got to admit, Shane didn't seem to accomplish a helluva lot at Calistoga."

"He was new in the business, Quinn. He was still learning."

"Peter, I interviewed Shane at his office there. He couldn't even tell me what kind of films he was planning to develop for Calistoga. I mean, shit, his job was to develop movies for TV, right?"

Peter nodded, staring at his untouched cup of coffee.

"And he couldn't describe one damn movie he had in development, Peter, not one!" If Shane had ever displayed any talent for the business, it must have been a slight one. Or else his drug use had erased it awfully quickly.

"I don't know. Maybe I'm kidding myself, but I just—"

"I'm sorry, Peter. You have to know how bad I feel about this."

Peter was quiet for a long time. Finally, he sipped his coffee; it had to be lukewarm by now. When he spoke again, his voice seemed to have lost all of its force. "You're still my friend, aren't you, Quinn?"

I patted his hand again. "Of course, Peter, you know that." I thought about all the years that had passed, all the years in which my former lover and I hadn't even spoken to each other. Not that there'd been any particular animosity between us when our affair ended. We'd simply gone on with our separate lives. I'd thought about Peter King now and then, of course. I wondered when he'd last thought about me. Before I found his dead son, that is.

"Will you do something for me?" he asked.

"Certainly, Peter. Name it."

"I—I have to know whether my boy was murdered, Quinn."

"But why would—"

"I don't know why. That's my point. Obviously, I didn't know shit about my own kid's life. Either he was big into drugs and I never saw it, or somebody had a reason to want him dead and I didn't even know he was in trouble. I—I can't live like this. My—Fuck it, Quinn, now I know how Rhett felt. Now I know how it feels when your soul bleeds."

Once more, I didn't know what to say. It hurt me to see someone I'd once loved in so much pain. Still, my own discomfort was nothing beside Peter's anguish and heartache. I felt my eyes grow moist and I swallowed hard before speaking. "What can I do to help you with this, Peter?" I asked.

"Just keep poking around, will you, Quinn? I already talked to the cops, and I know what they're thinking—I'm nothing but a grief-stricken father, a guy who doesn't know which end is up, a pain in the ass as far as they're concerned. They've already made up their minds—this is accidental death, just one more Hollywood druggie down the drain. But I—I'm not ready to buy that. Not yet."

"So you want me to poke around."

"Right. You can do it, Quinn, and nobody'll think anything of it. Me, everybody feels sorry for me, tells me what they think I want to hear. Hell, if I go and try to talk to those people at Calistoga, they're just going to sugarcoat things for me—I'm Shane's old man. But you're already doing a story about him, right? If you keep asking questions, people'll talk to you. They'll tell you things they'd never tell me."

"But what could I—"

"All I ask is that you find out whether my son was really an addict, Quinn. And maybe, I don't know—Maybe see if anybody'll give you a lead to his suppliers—if he had any."

"Wait a minute here, Peter. Asking around's one thing. Fingering Shane's drug source is something else. I'm not going to help you do anything stupid here."

"No, no, I'm not asking you to, Quinn. All I mean is I've got to know. Everything. You will help me, won't you?"

I wanted to tell Peter to go hire a private detective if he wanted somebody besides the cops to investigate his son's death. But, despite the Rolex on his wrist, I knew damn well he couldn't really afford one, not on the money he'd made in the past few years. And that funeral today had cost a buck or two. Knowing Veronica, Peter would be expected to pay at least half the tab for Shane's service and everything that went with it, even if she'd been the one to run up the bill, even if she'd made him stay away from the private gathering at her house afterward. I had no idea whether the youth had had any life insurance, either. Or if he did, who his beneficiary was. I simply couldn't see where Peter would get the money to pay a P.I.

"I'll see what I can find out," I promised reluctantly.

Peter tried to give birth to a smile, but it slipped off his lips, stillborn. "I knew I could count on you, Quinnie." His chin starting to quiver again, he signaled the waiter for the check.

When it came, I grabbed it before Peter could. "Compliments of the *Hollywood Star*," I told him. "Research for my article." But I placed my personal credit card across the bill.

Then I insisted that Peter leave his car in the city parking lot while I drove him home. He could worry about retrieving it later, after he sobered up.

The King family had enough tragedies to bear; I intended to see that another one didn't happen on the streets of Los Angeles today.

5

After lunch, I made a beeline back to the office. The time I'd spent at the funeral and lunch with Peter had set my work back several hours and I had to hustle if I was going to finish my baby moguls story on deadline. Before polishing what I'd already written, I phoned half a dozen people at Calistoga Pictures in search of someone—anyone besides Parker Kellerman—who'd admit being aware of Shane King's drug use.

"Sorry, I really can't comment on that," the dead man's secretary said in response to each of my questions. The woman on the phone sounded young, and I vaguely remembered a tiny redhead with buckteeth ushering me into Shane's office on the day I'd interviewed him at work.

"What do you mean, you can't comment?" I countered, feeling exasperated. "Either you knew Shane was using or you didn't. It's not a hard question."

She lowered her voice to a whisper. "Look, Ms. Collins, I talk to the press about Shane, I lose my job, it's that simple. I just can't help you." She hung up the phone in my ear.

My other calls to Calistoga personnel were equally revealing. Obviously, word was out at Shane's place of employment—nobody was to speak to the press about Shane or drugs, on penalty of immediate dismissal. In view of my looming deadline, I decided that angle of my story was probably superfluous anyway. Its point was the power the very young held in Hollywood, not that one of them had died. Besides, anything I was able to discover later on about Shane having a habit would fit nicely into the drugs-in-Hollywood story I'd been planning. So I spent the next hour rechecking facts about some of the other youthful execs I'd interviewed and rewriting what I already had. Then, with a sense of accomplishment, I filed my story.

What was left of the afternoon was eaten up by answering phone calls from agents and studio publicity people maneuvering to get their clients' names in this week's *Star*, plus bickering with Harry, who still was in a snit about plans for my next major feature. "Oh, for godsake, go sell some advertising!" I finally hollered at him in exasperation.

"When this town finds out you're telling their stockholders they're all a bunch of junkies, we won't have any ad buyers left!" he retorted. But he left my office.

I pushed my office door as far closed as its warped frame would allow. I needed a little privacy. Although I'd bombed out at Calistoga Pictures, there was at least one more thing I figured I could do to keep my promise to Peter. I grabbed the phone and dialed Detective Tracy Lewis' number. I caught him just as he was leaving for home.

"Nothing left to investigate there," Tracy told me. "Kid's death was obviously an accidental OD. Like I told you at the Malibu house, Quinn, this stuff happens all the time."

"But I talked to Shane's girlfriend and she confirms what he told me—he definitely wasn't a user," I countered. "His father says the same thing. Hell, Tracy, this kid hardly even touched alcohol, never mind shot heroin into his arm." I didn't mention Parker Kellerman's comments or the fact that a curtain of silence had been lowered at Calistoga Pictures.

I heard Tracy's exasperated sigh over the phone line and

felt myself stiffen. "You're not really that naive, Quinn," he told me. "Look, I never yet had an OD case from an affluent family where the relatives didn't express complete surprise. What're they gonna say, 'Yes, detective, I knew my child was using drugs but I'm so busy making money, I just didn't get around to doing anything about it?' The people you're talking to are protecting themselves. Either that, or Shane managed to fool them all."

"But his older brother died from an overdose, the brother Shane absolutely idolized. Ever since Rhett died, he was adamant about never going down that path himself."

"So what're you trying to tell me, that it *wasn't* an accident, that Shane King committed suicide?"

"Hell, no! I'm saying it's possible he was *murdered,* and I don't think you should close your investigation until you know for sure one way or the other."

"*Murdered?* That's really off the wall. Suicide, maybe. I might buy his killing himself if he was having problems, but do you really think it'd be a kindness to the family to push a suicide theory?"

Tracy was right about that, of course. And I had to admit—at least to myself, if not to the police—I'd certainly considered the possibility Shane's death was a suicide. Maybe he knew he was about to be fired from Calistoga Pictures and couldn't face the prospect of failure. Or maybe Tiffany's refusal to move in with him had pushed him over some psychological precipice. It's common knowledge that young people can lack perspective, that some of them kill themselves over setbacks an older person would take in stride. Still . . .

"You don't have any reason to think Shane was suicidal, do you, Tracy?" I asked.

"No," he admitted. "But I have far less reason to think

he was murdered. Just look at the facts: the kid died in his own Jacuzzi tub, the doors of his house were all locked, and a used syringe with heroine residue on it was lying next to his body. Nobody's prints on that syringe but young King's, by the way. I checked. So you tell me how he was murdered."

"By somebody he knew? Somebody who had a key to his house?" Tiffany, maybe, I thought. She might have had her own key. But why would she do that? She believed Shane was going to help her become a movie star.

"Sure," Tracy said. I could hear the derision in his deep voice. "And the murderer would have to be somebody Shane King would take off all his clothes and climb into the tub for, then let that person shoot him full of junk. If he really was the anti-drug fanatic you describe, Quinn, I'd love to hear your theory about how *that* chain of events came to pass."

I stared at the mess of papers on my wobbly old desk and felt my ire rising as Tracy shot down each of my arguments before I could even launch it. The cops obviously had given up on this case. "Your reluctance to continue investigating Shane's death wouldn't have anything to do with his rich Malibu neighbors, would it?" I asked, feeling bitchy and defensive. "I can certainly see where those folks wouldn't much care for the publicity attached to a murder investigation in their neighborhood."

Now it was Tracy's turn to bristle. "Look, Quinn, you're really beginning to irritate me. I'm trying to help you out here, so don't start questioning my motives. Read my lips—*the kid accidentally OD'd.* Only thing that might change my mind about that would be a suicide note with his signature on it, or having his tox screen come back clean—some nice, scientific evidence that it wasn't heroin that killed him after all."

"Okay," I said, putting on the brakes on my tongue before I managed to burn a valuable source. "I really do appreciate your help, Tracy. Just let me know when you get the tox screen back, will you?"

Telling myself I'd done as much as I could for now, I filed Shane King's death in the back of my mind until Thursday. In the rush to put the *Star* to bed for the week, I wrote two more features I'd already had in progress, double-checked my figures for a studio financial report, and reviewed three movies due to open in theaters within the next month. With the *Star*'s small staff, each of us has to wear more than one hat.

My uncle Teddy and our neighbor Sylvia accompanied me to one of the film screenings, but I attended the other two alone, sitting in the dark with the other reviewers and trying to guess their responses while they did their best to guess mine. Nobody likes to be the Lone Ranger as a reviewer, either loving a movie everybody else trashes, or hating one everyone else reveres. In these cases, however, the three offerings were so bland and derivative that I had trouble working up any enthusiasm in either direction. Or maybe it was just me. The events of the past week hadn't left me feeling very chipper.

On Thursday evening, with the week's paper finally on the presses, I nestled into my guesthouse and poured myself a glass of wine. Slumping down into my favorite chair, I figured I finally had an evening free to relax and read a book when my gaze fell on my answering machine. The little green light was flashing. Damn! I've never been able to ignore a summons of any kind. If I pretend I don't notice, I'm always convinced I'll die of curiosity.

Disgusted with my lack of self-control, I got up out of

my chair and pushed PLAY.

"Hi, Quinnie, it's me, Peter," I heard. The man sounded tired, and maybe a little drunk again as well. "Look, I don't wanna bug you, but I wondered if you'd learned anything more about Shane. I just—Well, you know. Call me, huh?"

I felt instantly guilty. I hadn't done a single thing about Shane since talking to Detective Lewis. At least I could speak to a few more of Shane's friends, I decided, as a favor to Peter. Certainly I had to make it look like I'd really tried. I picked up the phone and dialed Tiffany Novotny's number in Palms. Surely she would have the names and phone numbers of Shane's current crowd.

When an older woman answered the phone, I identified myself and asked to speak to Tiffany. "Oh, Miss Collins," the woman gushed. "How nice to hear from you. I'm Emma Novotny, Tiffany's aunt. I read your stories in the *Hollywood Star* all the time, and I can't tell you how thrilled Tiffany is that you interviewed her."

"I'm happy to hear that," I said, feeling guiltier. Tiffany wouldn't be quite so thrilled when the *Star* hit the stands tomorrow and she found out her big interview had been condensed to a couple of her comments about Shane. All the more reason I should talk to her tonight. "May I speak with her, please?"

"Oh, I guess you didn't hear," Emma Novotny said. "The most wonderful thing happened—it's almost like that interview with you turned her career right around. She got a job!"

"What kind of job?" I asked, feigning polite interest. I hoped Tiffany wouldn't ask me to run a publicity piece about this for her.

"*Acting,* of course, in a film being shot on location." Emma Novotny's tone let me know that Tiffany couldn't possibly consider any other kind of work. No selling cosmetics or typing business letters for this girl—she was a beauty contest winner! "Tiff's already left town," her aunt added.

My brow furrowed. Even as exhausted as I was, this sounded strange to me, unless Tiffany had been hired as a last-minute replacement for another actress who'd been fired or taken ill. Generally, actors aren't hired and already working on location within the next day or two. "What's the name of the picture?" I asked, trying to keep the skeptical tone out of my voice. No point in alarming the girl's aunt.

There was a pause on the line. "*Night—Night* something or other, I think," she said finally. "I'm not really sure. Tiff says it's only a working title, anyway."

"Do you know the star, or the director?"

"Sorry. I think it's a pretty low budget film, nobody I ever heard of. But it's a start for her, right?"

"Everybody's got to start somewhere," I agreed, hoping Tiffany hadn't gotten herself involved in some sort of porn flick. "What's the production company?"

"Sorry. I think Tiff told me the name, but it didn't mean anything to me. It wasn't Universal or Disney or any of the big studios. It's some sort of independent production, I guess."

I made a mental note to check the list of active productions when I got into the office in the morning. "Know where they're shooting?"

"That much I do know—up in Big Sur." Big Sur certainly wasn't usual porn movie territory—most of those pictures are shot in converted warehouses around the L.A. area. As far as I knew, Big Sur didn't have either a warehouse or a sound stage, so this had to be completely an outdoor shoot. "Tiff left early so she could spend a little time with her folks on the farm before she has to report to the set," Mrs. Novotny told me. "They're right outside Salinas."

She gave me the phone number for Tiffany's parents but, when I dialed it, there was no answer, not even a machine to take a message. For a fleeting instant, I was envious of old-fashioned farm life, the kind of simple existence where people could still be out of touch for hours at a time, where they didn't have to deal with cell phones, voice mail, fax machines or computers. I pictured myself sitting on the broad porch of a big white house, watching the sun setting over my very own lush green fields, the twitter of birds providing the only break in the thick, relaxing silence.

But my reverie didn't last for long—I knew that kind of life would bore a Type A like me to tears inside a weekend.

I couldn't reach Tiffany, but Peter might know at least some of Shane's current friends. I dialed my old boyfriend's number from memory and reassured him I hadn't forgotten my promise, that indeed I'd been working on getting the information he wanted.

He was able to give me the names of the two young men who were Shane's best friends in high school, but he didn't know any of the guys Shane had hung out with more recently, not even their names. Nor did he know where Jason and Bart, the high school buddies, now lived. He still had their parents' phone numbers in his address book, however. At least that was something.

No, he hadn't seen either Jason or Bart at the funeral, Peter told me. "Probably had work conflicts or were out of town or something," he added. I felt a pang of sympathy for this father whose son's "best friends" of only a few years ago hadn't even bothered to attend his memorial service.

Tomorrow would be plenty soon enough to call them, I

told myself, fully expecting to learn nothing new from them, anyway. Besides, now that I'd talked to Peter again, certainly I'd bought myself some time.

I switched off the ringer on my phone, settled back into my easy chair, took a sip of my wine, and picked up my novel. At least for a few hours, I could pretend I was on a mini-vacation in something resembling the carefree world I imagined Tiffany Novotny was now revisiting.

"Shane? Yeah, I heard about it, that he died," Bart Amundson told me. "Tough break." A tall young man with a shock of fair hair and a thick ginger beard, he was leaning against a shiny black Ford Explorer with a sullen, I-couldn't-care-less expression on his face. His demeanor had changed in a flash as soon as he discovered I wasn't looking to trade in my old Mercedes on the new SUV he wanted to sell me, that instead all I wanted was some information about Shane King.

I'd started my morning by calling the phone numbers Peter had given me the night before. Jason Wilsky was living in England, his mother told me, her voice filled with pride. He was studying international economics at Oxford University. She was certain her son had not been in contact with Shane King for years. "They were tight in high school, but the boys just drifted apart after they graduated," she told me. "You know how it is—they grow up, end up with different goals, different friends." It was obvious Mrs. Wilsky felt her son's goals, and probably his current friends as well, were far superior to Shane's. She probably was right.

My second phone call held more promise. I learned that Bart Amundson now worked at his father's car dealership, located just a few blocks from my office. I decided to drop by and talk to him on my way into work.

It wasn't hard to tell which of the two salesmen in the Ford-Lincoln-Mercury showroom was Bart Amundson. The second man was middle-aged and portly, with an air of low expectations about him. Bart, on the other hand, was still young enough to be a go-getter.

Right up until I told him the real reason I'd stopped by.

"When was the last time you saw Shane?" I asked Bart now. I was confused by his obvious callousness in the face of his friend's death.

"What difference does that make? He's dead, right?" Bart's eyes flicked away from me and he watched through the showroom window as a young couple wandered onto the car lot. He obviously was sizing them up as prospective customers, giving them the same once-over he'd given me when I'd pulled into the curb and approached the dealership a few minutes earlier.

"Shane's dad doesn't believe he overdosed," I told him. No point in beating around the bush, I figured, not when Bart seemed ready to cut me off and bolt toward hotter prospects at any moment. "I promised Peter King I'd talk with some of Shane's friends, see if they could tell me anything about his habits."

"Couldn't prove anything one way or the other by me," Bart said, still not making eye contact. "Shane and me, we started going our own way after high school. Then, when he got that big job at Calistoga, that was the end. He got this attitude, like he was too good for his old buds. Started acting like we were dog shit he stepped in or something."

"Just because he got a job in the movie business?"

"How the hell do I know why? Shane had been acting weird for a while, like he had bigger plans than the rest of us, like me working for my dad here didn't qualify me for his fucking social circle. Or maybe even to breathe the same air. Who the hell knows what was going through that thick head of his."

"So that's why you didn't go to Shane's funeral."

Bart turned back to me and sneered. "Hey, I was busy working," he said defensively, "just like I am now." He turned on his heel and headed through the showroom's glass door and toward the young couple, who were now reading the price sticker on the window of a new Excursion. "Sorry I can't help you," Bart shot over his shoulder.

Yeah, right, I thought as I followed him outside. I could see he was all broken up about it.

Had Shane snubbed all his old friends, I wondered as I climbed into the Mercedes and turned the key in ignition, or had he singled out Bart? Dumping his old buddies could have been a sign Shane was using drugs, that he was actively distancing himself from anyone who might discover his secret habit. Or maybe he simply felt he'd outgrown his old high school gang.

Jason Wilsky's mom was right, I thought—as we grow older, how many of us really keep the same friends we had when we were kids? Although I still had sporadic contact with a few people I'd known in high school and college—most of them, like me, connected in some way to show business—I couldn't claim a single one of them as a close friend today.

I glanced back at the car lot before pulling into traffic. The sullen expression had completely disappeared from Bart Amundson's face. Now he was all smiles as he launched into his heavy-duty sales pitch for one of the biggest sports utility vehicles ever built.

When I arrived at the office, Harry was sitting on the

edge of Lucy's desk staring at the door. He looked like somebody had just punched him in the stomach. "What's the matter?" I asked, concerned that Harry's volatile nature had finally propelled him into a heart attack.

"They're suing us," he murmured, his face ashen. "They're actually suing us! This is gonna be the final nail in the *Star*'s coffin. We're gonna sink faster than Sandra Bullock's last picture."

"What're you talking about? Who's suing us?"

Harry's defeated eyes rose to meet mine. I detected a flash of anger, but it was gone again as quickly as it had appeared. "Pierce Ireland, Quinn. That little prick and his lawyer are suing us for fifteen million fucking dollars."

Lucy flinched and looked away, as she always does when anybody uses profanity around her. In this office—hell, in this town—that's about umpteen times each and every day.

I began to feel a little sick. "What the—Why on earth would Pierce Ireland sue us?" Ireland was the young director, all of twenty-two years old, who'd been entrusted with Consolidated Pictures' newest action film. I'd interviewed him and half a dozen others working on the project for my baby moguls article.

A little life, in the form of anger, began to flow back into Harry. "Because of what *you* wrote," he told me. "Says you libeled him when you said he was fifteen million over budget by the time he was halfway through the shoot. Now the studio's threatening to fire him off the picture. Claims you ruined his career, so he's going to ruin yours. Problem is, he'll be ruining everybody else's around here, too."

I had a strong feeling Harry wouldn't object a whole lot to Ireland's wrecking my career, as long as he didn't step on Harry's own toes. "Hey, at least the kid read this week's

Star as soon as it hit the stands," I said, making a feeble attempt at humor.

"Maybe if we agree to print a retraction," Harry suggested, "and a sincere apol—"

"Screw that!" I shouted. "I'm not retracting one word of my story, and I sure as hell am *not* going to apologize to that little pipsqueak." Now I was getting angry myself. I'd worked my butt off on that piece and I didn't appreciate Harry's obvious willingness to roll over on me before I even had a chance to defend what I'd written.

"But—"

"But nothing, Harry. You know I never write a word without plenty of research to back it up. Want to see the accounting spreadsheet I got from my source on Ireland's picture? That fifteen million figure is actually low. Truth is, they're closer to seventeen million in the hole by now. You'll find more red on that shoot's books than on the victims in your average slasher picture."

"You've got actual figures?" Harry managed to look both sheepish and hopeful at the same time. "From Ireland's accountants?"

"Damn right, I do, and I'll be more than happy to fax a copy of everything I've got to the little pissant's lawyer."

"So maybe they won't sue us after all. Because right now just defending a lawsuit, even if we win in the end, could bankrupt us."

"Or maybe we should let them go ahead and file their damn suit," I suggested, "get ourselves a little free publicity from all our gloating competitors, maybe even a few lines in the *Times*. *Then* we can produce the facts and get them to drop their suit and apologize to us. Get us even more free publicity."

Harry pressed his fingertips against his temples. "Just get

me the fucking spreadsheet, Quinn. We don't have time for games."

An hour later, after Harry had faxed his cover letter threatening to countersue, along with a copy of the financial figures I'd obtained to Pierce Ireland's attorney, he barged into my office. "That's done," he said, beginning to pace the small space. "Let's just hope it works."

"Of course, it will work," I told him. "They're just bluffing. Intimidation's this town's favorite game. Can't let them intimidate us or we're all dead meat." Harry knew as well as I did that image was everything in Hollywood. This is a place where people who don't have the price of tomorrow's breakfast finance designer wardrobes and liposuction treatments on credit cards. The rules of the game are strict—as soon as somebody looks the least bit tired or old or hungry or frightened, the vultures begin to circle and he's finished. The last thing the *Hollywood Star* could afford was to appear intimidated. That would kill us far faster than any lawsuit.

Harry glanced down at my desk. "What's that you're working on?"

"A list of night spots catering to young people in the industry, and the names of a few of contacts who might be able to give me some fresh leads." Some of these joints were now out of vogue, I'd discovered in my computer search of back issues of the *Times* and a few show business periodicals. Seems having a celebrity overdose in your nightclub, or even on the sidewalk out front, could be bad for business.

"That drugs-in-Hollywood story again?"

I straightened up in my chair. "Not again," I told him, "still."

Harry sighed audibly and plopped down into a chair. "I

think you should take some time off, Quinn," he said, his face rapidly turning crimson.

"Where's *that* coming from?" I asked, but I already knew.

"What's with you and this drugs thing? We're not close enough to being sued already?" he asked. He shook his head in what appeared to be a combination of astonishment and disbelief.

"Intimidation," I reminded him. "We're finished if we run scared."

"Look, Quinn, you discovered a dead body just a few days ago. That'd be traumatic enough under any circumstances. But this was somebody you know, somebody whose family you know."

"And your point is?"

"You're not thinking clearly. I think you need to take some time off, maybe even take a session or two with a shrink, talk it out before—"

"A *shrink?* Are you nuts, Harry, or just being insulting?"

"What's insulting about seeing a shrink? Half the people I know see shrinks. Hell, *I* see a shrink."

Harry was right, of course. Seeing a shrink is another Hollywood status symbol. I just resented his conclusion that the only reason I wanted to write my drug story was because I'd become mentally unhinged by finding Shane King's dead body.

"No, Harry. N-O."

"Just a few days off, Quinn, that's all I'm suggesting. We'll run next week's edition four pages short if we have to. We've done it before."

"What part of no don't you understand?" I snapped. "Now, if you don't mind, I've got work to do."

Harry rolled his eyes, but he stood up.

"Just think about it, okay?" he shot over his shoulder as

he left my office.

I went back to my notes, then began calling a few young actors who owed me a favor. I figured they might be able to point me toward the current action spots. Billy Gee, a six-foot-two blond hunk who was into weightlifting, was the only one to answer his phone.

"You start poking around that scene, everybody's gonna think you're a narc, Quinn," Billy warned me when I asked him for advice. "Or somebody's mom."

"Thanks for the compliment," I said, feeling suddenly ancient.

"Just telling you like it is. Anybody over thirty, forget it. Might as well be wearing a badge. Lucky if they let you in."

At least he hadn't implied I looked over forty or even fifty. I had no illusions about passing for under thirty anymore, no matter what color I dyed my hair, but I still hoped I could shave a few years off my real age without looking pathetic. "Maybe you could visit a few of these clubs with me," I suggested. "You look young enough to get us in." Billy was thirty-four, but he'd had a movie role as a college student just last year and he'd looked very convincing. "You'd fit in, easy."

I thought I heard the beginning of a laugh at the other end of the phone line, but I must have been wrong. Billy, like most actors, wasn't exactly the brightest bulb on the tree, but surely he wasn't stupid enough to burn as important a publicity source as the *Hollywood Star.*

"I—I—" he stammered through a choking sound.

"I'll pay," I reassured him. "Expense account." I don't give up easily.

"It's just that—" There was such a long pause I could almost hear Billy's two or three mental gears grinding. "—I—I'm going out of town this weekend, Quinn, that's the problem. To Tahoe. I'd cancel, but it's my parents wedding anniversary and I promised them I'd be there."

Billy hailed from Philadelphia, not Tahoe, but undoubtedly he'd forgotten he'd told me that. His obviously phony excuse was probably lifted from the last movie script he'd read, or from the dialogue on some TV soap opera. I heard a light knock on my office door, followed by a squeak as Lucy pushed it open. I gestured for her to enter. She looked troubled, but then Lucy often looks troubled.

"Never mind, Billy, it was just a thought," I said, letting him off the hook. I couldn't really blame the guy. It wouldn't do his acting career much good to be seen with me while I was prowling the local club scene. Not if I was researching an article that might make people who could offer him work look bad. "Thanks for the advice."

I hung up and turned my attention to our secretary. She was gripping a piece of paper tightly in her freckled hand.

"Thought you'd want to see this," she said, nervously thrusting the paper at me. "Just came in on the AP wire. It's that girl you interviewed, isn't it?"

Confused, I grabbed the copy and read it quickly:

> "A young woman who plunged to her death from a Big Sur cliff Wednesday night has been identified as Tiffany Novotny, 20, of Los Angeles.
>
> "Sheriff's deputies said that Novotny, driving a late model red Miata convertible, apparently lost control of her vehicle half a mile south of Rocky Point sometime after dark Wednesday. Her car was spotted by hikers early Thursday morning when . . ."

I glanced up and nodded slowly to Lucy. "Shane King's girlfriend," I told her. "She was supposed to be working on a movie up there." Despite the warm sunlight pouring through the office window, I shivered.

"And now this girl's dead, too, just like poor Shane." Lucy, who'd never laid eyes on either Tiffany Novotny or Shane King, looked like she was about to cry.

"Seems very odd, doesn't it, Lucy?"

"Milton and I drove that Big Sur highway once," she told me. Milton Flint—she never referred to him as Milt or Miltie, always Milton—was Lucy's late husband. "Never been so scared in my life, all those cliffs and hills and curves, and the highway's so *narrow*, too. Poor little Tiffany was probably upset about Shane, distracted, you know how it is when someone you love dies. Certainly would be easy enough to drive a little too fast, lose control of your car, especially on a treacherous stretch of road like that."

"Looks like she was driving the car Shane gave her," I said, feeling more and more uneasy. Maybe Tiffany had been upset, like Lucy suggested. But, if so, she'd certainly hidden her grief awfully well at Shane's funeral and, frankly, I didn't think she was that good an actress. Or maybe she was just a really bad driver. Or perhaps she'd been under the influence of something, possibly trying out some of those drugs she'd claimed Shane wouldn't let her touch.

Still, if there was anything to Peter King's hunch that his son might have been murdered, Tiffany's death seemed terribly convenient. If she'd known something incriminating, that knowledge had died with her. Was her death really an accident? I wondered. But apparently the local police thought so.

I skimmed the remainder of the brief story. It didn't contain a word to indicate there was any criminal investigation going on at the crash site. As far as AP and the police seemed to be concerned, this was just another unfortunate traffic accident, something that happened in Big Sur three or four times each month. The story probably wouldn't even have made the statewide newswire, except that Tiffany had ties both to Monterey County and L.A. There was no mention of her connection to Shane King.

"Thanks for spotting this, Lucy," I said, staring at the piles of notes on my desk. Suddenly, cruising the hot night spots in search of industry druggies seemed far less urgent than it had just a few minutes ago. Billy Gee was undoubtedly right—I wouldn't get my story, at least not in the way I'd planned to research it. Besides, who would I get to go with me, Uncle Teddy? Talk about looking like somebody's parents! I decided I'd better think of another way to get my drugs-in-Hollywood story. Surely there was nothing urgent about it; it could wait a week or two.

Tiffany Novotny's death, on the other hand, seemed to cry out for immediate investigation.

I began to scoop my notes into a pile. "Lucy," I said, as she headed back to her desk in the outer office.

She turned and looked back at me inquiringly.

"Tell Harry I've decided to take his advice, will you?" I said. "I'm going to take a few days off, get my head together."

"Excellent idea, dear," she said, her face brightening. "All this stress can't be good for your health. You work too hard. Little break will do you a world of good."

When she'd left my office, I reviewed my notes on the interview I'd done with Tiffany and refreshed my memory about the name of her agent. I picked up the phone and dialed the small agency that had represented her.

"Tiffany Novotny?" the receptionist responded when I asked her about where the young actress was currently working. "Hold a minute, will you? I'm not sure Creative Talent still represents her."

I waited on the line for two or three minutes, knowing full well that this fly-by-night agency probably didn't have more than a dozen clients, all of whom were beginners in the business. How difficult could it be for this receptionist to remember whether Tiffany remained on their roster? And did they already know Tiffany was dead?

"Hello, Ms. Collins? I was right. Tiffany Novotny is no longer with Creative Talent."

"What agency is she with now?"

"Dunno. Didn't say where she was going when she left."

"So when did she quit your agency?" Apparently Creative Talent did not know their former client was dead, and I had no intention of being the one to inform them.

"Sorry, I'm not at liberty to say anything except she's no longer with us."

"And you honestly don't know who's representing her now? It's really important that I reach her agent."

"Sorry, Ms. Collins, can't help you." The line went dead.

So Creative Talent hadn't gotten Tiffany the acting job in Big Sur and, if her old agency knew who did, nobody there was itching to tell me. Creative Talent's reason for being so secretive could be nefarious, I thought, but more likely, it was simply raw resentment. Understandably, small-time agents tend to feel rejected when their clients fire them in favor of somebody with more clout. That's a common career move for actors, directors, and writers on their way up, but one that invariably causes hard feelings.

I checked our list of films in production one more time, but there still was no location shoot listed for Big Sur, nor was there a current project with the word "night" in its title.

A quick call to the Monterey County Film Commission confirmed my fears. "We've got a Toyota commercial scheduled to shoot at Bixby Bridge later this month," the commission representative told me, "but nothing in Big Sur right now."

My bad feeling about Tiffany Novotny's fate increased.

I spent the next hour doing a quick edit job on a few press releases that we could use as filler for the next edition of the *Star* if my journey north took longer than the weekend. Then I grabbed my tape recorder and a California map and stuffed them into my briefcase along with my camera and notepads.

As I rushed out the door, I reassured myself that, even if I was on a wild goose chase, nobody else would know about it unless I learned something useful. Besides, there was no better place to clear my head than the rocky coastline of central California.

6

I drove north on Highway 101, losing precious time in the usual traffic jam around Santa Barbara, then opened up on the road between Goleta and Pismo Beach, watching out for the CHP in my rear view mirror. I turned westward toward the sea on Highway 1 when it split off from 101 in San Luis Obispo, and hugged the coastline when the highway turned northward past Morro Bay and Cambria.

By the time I'd passed Hearst Castle and reached the southern end of the Big Sur coast, it was already growing dark. Dark in Big Sur is *dark*—pitch black on a moonless night. There's no such thing as a street light in that part of the world, and the dimly lit houses and businesses are few and far between. Frequently, you can hardly tell where the road ends and the abyss begins.

As I drove the road along the edge of the cliff, I could see how a young, inexperienced driver like Tiffany might make a wrong move and plunge into the Pacific below. Maybe, I thought, her death really was an accident.

It took me almost another hour to reach Nepenthe, the funky restaurant built on hilltop land once owned by Orson Welles and Rita Hayworth. It was clear I wasn't going to get a look at the spot where Tiffany's little red Miata had gone off the highway and crashed onto the rocks below before tomorrow morning and, by now, I was both tired and hungry. I pulled into Nepenthe's parking lot and climbed the steep stairway to the restaurant. It felt good to stretch my legs after all those hours in the car.

I chatted up the waitress, a long-haired waif of a girl called Sunny, as I ate an overpriced hamburger with a side of coleslaw. When I asked her advice, Sunny suggested I stay the night at the rustic Big Sur Lodge, which was only another mile or so up the road. I had a choice of the Lodge, she told me, or one of the more prestigious places—the Post Ranch Inn or Ventana—that charge their customers a minimum of four hundred dollars a night. Otherwise, I would have to drive on to Carmel, another forty-five minutes north. I decided to try the nearby, much lower-cost Big Sur Lodge.

"Know anything about a movie being shot in Big Sur?" I asked Sunny as I scooped up the last bite of coleslaw on my plate. "Supposed to be called *Night*-something."

Sunny shook her head. "Not that I heard about." She called over her shoulder to the bartender. "Hey, Chuck, hear if there's a movie being shot around here?"

The tall, rangy bartender looked up from wiping the bar top and shook his head, his pony tail brushing against his bony shoulders. "Nope. If there was a movie, their people'd end up in here—they always do—and I'd know about it. No Hollywood folks around for at least a year now."

"Thanks, anyway," I said.

"Maybe they're on their way," the waitress suggested, sounding hopeful. "If they're going to make a movie and they need people to be extras, I could work days. My shift here doesn't start until six."

"If I find the film company, I'll be sure to let you know," I told her.

I asked both Sunny and Chuck what they knew about the car accident that had killed Tiffany Novotny, but unlike a production company shooting a film, auto accidents were common occurrences in this neighborhood. As such, they didn't draw much notice, unless one of the locals was involved.

"Always some tourist misjudging that highway," Chuck said, summing up the situation succinctly. "One wrong move and you're fish food."

I wondered how many of those dead tourists had tanked up on liquor Chuck had poured before they ventured back out onto that treacherous road.

I left a generous tip and headed north toward the Big Sur Lodge.

Rustic was definitely the operative word for the Lodge. For the first time in my entire life, I slept in a log cabin *sans* telephone, TV, or radio. As far as this place was concerned, Hollywood didn't even exist, which I found rather refreshing, at least for a little while. My accommodations offered a generous ration of rural charm, along with indoor plumbing and a wood-burning fireplace. If I hadn't been so tired from my drive, I might have started a fire and warmed myself in front of its crackling flames, pretending I lived in a much earlier, simpler time before movies even existed. Instead, I quickly crawled into bed.

As I lay there, I felt suddenly deafened by the silence that enveloped me. After the noise of Los Angeles, to which I'd been accustomed since birth, this seemed downright eerie. But as my ears adjusted, I began to distinguish the slight rustling sound of the breeze in the treetops and the distant call of a owl.

I slept soundly, awakening the next morning to the twitter of birds and sunlight streaming through the cabin's windows.

It wasn't hard to find the spot where Tiffany's little red Miata went over the cliff—there was still a piece of yellow police tape hanging across the broken section of the traffic barrier at the scene near Rocky Creek Bridge. I pulled off the road and parked.

As I approached the place where the low rusty metal railing was bent and broken, I had a quick visceral reaction. Thank God I hadn't eaten breakfast. I wondered whether my nausea was because this was where young Tiffany had died, or because my own parents had met their end in the same way.

I didn't even know exactly where in Malibu my folks' car had skidded off the pavement into the ocean on that rainy night so long ago. I was only a toddler at the time. Still, Uncle Teddy had to know the spot where my folks died. I realized now that I'd never even asked him about it. At some level, I guess I didn't want to know where it happened—it was enough to know and accept that it did. I hadn't want to be reminded of my loss every time I drove past the fatal spot.

Even though I have no real memory of my parents, I harbor what you might call imagined memories, full-blown fantasies of what I dream it was like when we were all together. My idea of a loving, Leave-It-to-Beaver existence that surely would never hold up to close scrutiny.

Luckily, there was little traffic at this early hour and what existed was heading south, mainly tourists on a day's outing in Big Sur, so I had this highway turnout to myself.

Standing behind what was left of the road barrier, I swallowed hard and peered out over the edge of the cliff. I could make out bright red marks on two or three rocks jutting out between where I stood and the water churning far below, probably spots where the Miata's paint had scraped off during the little car's plunge to the shoreline. The red scars were all that remained now; Tiffany's car had already been removed.

I wondered how the highway patrol would have accomplished such a task. It would require a helicopter, I figured. Whatever was left of the Miata was probably in some insurance company's junkyard by now. There was no police presence here, nothing other than the yellow plastic tape whipping in the morning breeze to prove they'd even been here, so this fatality obviously was being treated as a routine traffic accident.

I stood back from the cliff's edge and looked at the highway in both directions. I could see that Tiffany had to have been traveling north on the inland side of the highway, heading toward Carmel, to hit the barrier at this angle and with enough force to break through it and plunge over the edge. Had she fallen asleep at the wheel, swerved across the oncoming traffic lane, and crashed through the barrier?

If she'd been traveling in the other direction, she'd have been driving uphill, necessarily at a much slower speed, and she'd have hit the barrier with far less force. From that direction and at a low speed, at worst the Miata would have slid into the protective railing, perhaps bending but not breaking it, and come to a halt. The car might have been severely damaged, but Tiffany would still be alive.

Unless she'd already been dead before her car hit that barrier.

There were so many tire marks in the dirt here that there was no way of telling which might have been made by Tiffany's car. Two and a half days had passed since the crash, and there'd been rescue vehicles and personnel here, as well as possibly dozens of tourists, trampling all over the scene. Even if I were an expert, which I'm definitely not, I probably couldn't have learned anything here at this late date.

I crossed the highway and walked uphill along its inland shoulder, feeling the steep grade pulling at my calves and knees. There's a good reason doctors recommend swimming as the best exercise after a certain age, and I was beginning to think I'd pretty well reached that age.

By the time I reached the first curve in the road and another small turnout, I was huffing and puffing and my leg muscles burned. When I'd caught my breath, I turned for a moment and surveyed the spectacular Big Sur coastline behind me. Green and gold hills dropped straight toward the blue and green Pacific. Wisps of morning fog nestled in the crevasses between the hills. Pelicans swooped toward the water on their fishing expeditions while gulls screeched from the shoreline. The peaceful scene displayed no hint that a young woman had lost her life here so recently.

The Miata had to have ventured over the road's center line somewhere between where I stood and where it had gone off the cliff, that much was clear. If it had veered wrong any higher uphill, I realized, wiping my brow, it would have landed in an entirely different spot.

Like the lower turnout where I'd left my car, this one was covered with both tire tracks and footprints. There was nothing I could learn from it, except that it was used frequently.

Yet as I walked back downhill to my Mercedes, I was struck by one possibly important observation—there were no fresh skid marks on the highway's sun-baked surface. Surely, I thought, if Tiffany had been awake at the wheel of her car, she would have slammed on her brakes as she realized she was about to head off the road.

Either she was not awake, I had to conclude, or she'd fully intended driving off this cliff to her death.

★ ★ ★ ★ ★

I had a late breakfast at a small cafe in Carmel, then headed east on Highway 68 to Salinas and turned south on Highway 101.

I drove past fields ripe with lettuce and broccoli, the latter's odor pungent in the air. It was much warmer here than in Big Sur; I switched on my car's air conditioner. As I checked the odometer to make sure I didn't miss my turnoff—the farm where Tiffany's parents lived was three miles inland from Highway 101 and several miles south of the city—I passed field after field of ripe strawberries. I saw dozens of dark-skinned men in sweat-stained shirts and jeans stooping over the bright red berries, filling green cardboard boxes that would head for market later in the day. At the edge of the largest field stood an ancient school bus, now painted white, and a portable toilet.

Not a whole lot had changed since John Steinbeck wrote about this part of the country half a century ago, I thought. Migrant workers were still doing brutally hard physical work for subsistence wages. The only real difference was that now they traveled north to California from Mexico to work in these fields, instead of west from Oklahoma.

At the driveway I was seeking, I found two mailboxes mounted on a single wrought-iron post, one marked "Olson" and the other "Novotny." I turned in, drove the full length of a city block, and parked in front of a huge modern house with a wide, well-shaded porch on which sat matching redwood rocking chairs. I was impressed. This farm was no small-time operation.

A pretty blond woman in her late thirties answered my knock at the front door. "Mr. and Mrs. Novotny?" she said in response to my query. "Oh, no, not here. You want the foreman's house out back." She glanced at her watch.

"Shirley's probably home, but Oscar should still be in the fields, this time of day." Apparently Tiffany's father wasn't entitled to take bereavement leave.

The woman indicated that I should drive around the back of her house, then travel a few hundred yards farther down the road. "Just continue on past the field workers' housing complex," she told me. "Can't miss it."

I thanked her and got back into my car. As I rounded the back of the big house, the road turned from asphalt to dirt and I could feel every hard rut as I passed what the blonde had called the worker's housing complex. A row of run-down shacks was more like it. Shuddering at the thought of being forced to live in one of these squalid huts, I had to wonder whether they even had indoor plumbing and electricity. Next to these depressing dumps, the Big Sur Lodge looked like the Taj Mahal.

The Novotnys' house was far more appealing than the workers' hovels, but still a far cry from the owner's digs. It was two stories high, with a rickety porch and peeling white paint trimmed in faded blue. The single area of real cheerfulness was at the east side of the house, a huge flower garden filled with roses of every hue, alongside what looked to me like geraniums and some variety of daisy. I also spotted a bushy plant whose flowers were a lovely shade of indigo, but I had no idea what it might be called. I have the world's blackest thumb when it comes to gardening—ever since I watered his African violets into an untimely death, Uncle Teddy's been claiming I could kill *plastic* flowers if given a chance, and he's undoubtedly right. I'm definitely no expert on plant varieties.

Looking at this place, I had a new insight into why Tiffany had dreamed of becoming a movie star, and why the prospect of marrying the richest, most powerful man she could possibly snare had been so enticing to her. Where she'd grown up, she'd been subjected daily to the specter of the farm owners' wealth juxtaposed against the dire warning of what lay in store for people who lacked financial resources. If her parents' circumstances weren't depressing enough, she had only to look down the road to observe the migrant workers' sad lives.

The woman who answered the door to this house looked worn out, her eyes ringed with red. She'd obviously been crying.

"Miss Collins?" she said through the screen door. I'd called earlier to let her know I'd be stopping by to see her.

"Right," I said. "Call me Quinn. You must be Mrs. Novotny."

She nodded. "I'm Shirley. Come on in. I've got some ice tea in the fridge if you'd like some."

"That would be awfully nice, Shirley. But, please, don't go to any trouble on my account."

"No trouble." She led me into the kitchen and pulled out a chair for me to sit at the table. Like the outside of the house, the kitchen hadn't been updated in at least thirty years. The counters were old-fashioned, deeply worn yellow Formica and there was no dishwasher in sight, just a plastic drainer on the counter next to the sink. The ancient refrigerator was a shade I think was known as coppertone, a style that was popular sometime in the sixties. Still, Shirley Novotny'd obviously done as much as possible to make her home cheerful, adding blue-and-white checked gingham curtains to the windows and a bouquet of fresh flowers for the table.

"Looks like you're quite a gardener," I said, leaning over and smelling the flowers.

"Just a hobby. Passes the time while Oscar's in the fields

with the men." She set our tea glasses, along with a bowl of sugar, on the table, which was covered with a crisply ironed blue cloth. "You said you knew my Tiffany?" Her dark eyes welled up again as she spoke her daughter's name. Her skin was darker than her daughter's—I wondered if she had some Hispanic blood—but they shared the same dark hair and eyes.

"Tiffany and I met fairly recently," I told her, taking a sip of tea. It had a minty after-taste, perhaps from an herb she'd grown in her garden. "I interviewed her for a story I wrote for my paper, the *Hollywood Star*. It was about young movers and shakers in show business, and one of my main subjects was Shane King, the young man Tiffany'd been dating. So when I heard what happened to her, I really felt terrible."

"Shane King, yes." Shirley's gaze dropped to her hands, which were circling her glass. Her knuckles were white. "Tiffany told us about this Shane kid, said he was in love with her."

"She told me the same thing. Unfortunately, Shane died shortly before Tiffany's accident. The last time I saw her was at Shane's funeral."

Shirley wiped a tear from her cheek. "From what she said, that boy was crazy about her. I mean, why wouldn't he be, a pretty girl like Tiffany? I don't think she was ready to settle down, though, not for good. She said Shane was pressuring her to move in with him and she was feeling a little bit smothered." She smoothed the front of her yellow cotton shirt as if afraid her tears had stained it. "My Tiffany had so much to look forward to, being in the movies and everything that goes with that kind of life, and she was still very young, much too young to think about settling down with one man and getting married."

I wondered how old Shirley was when she married Oscar Novotny. Probably not much older than Tiffany, I guessed. Clearly she had wanted something else for her daughter.

"I mean, who would figure a girl from here—" Shirley gestured around the house. "—a girl from a strawberry farm south of Salinas, would end up in Hollywood, would maybe even get to be a movie star?"

It seemed inappropriate for me to express my opinion that Tiffany's chances of ending up a movie star were roughly the same as the proverbial snowball's chances of surviving hell. After all, the poor girl was dead. The least I could do was let her mother enjoy her fantasy, so I kept my lip zipped.

"Now . . . now we're planning her funeral." Her chin began to quiver again.

"Do—do you have other children, Shirley?" I asked, hoping to switch to a less depressing subject.

"No . . . no. Tiffany's all I ever had. My husband, Oscar, he's older than me, already forty-three when our little girl was born. Not that he didn't dote on Tiffany, he did, but having a toddler under foot was hard for him. After all day in the fields, he'd come home exhausted, wanting to sit and relax, enjoy a beer or two, not listen to a little girl yammering at him. That's what he always called it—yammering. So we—we never had any more kids after Tiffany was born."

"Must have been a lonely childhood for her, living way out here."

"Tiffany? Oh, no, that girl was always real social. Played with the migrants' kids when she was little, and later she had her friends at school. Real popular." Shirley took a sip of her tea and gazed out the window at the mountains in the distance. "I think she was happy to leave, though, when Oscar's brother and his wife said she could come and live with them down in L.A., try her hand at acting."

So Tiffany had spent her youth playing with the migrants' children on this farm. I wondered where she'd developed her Valley-girl accent. It seemed more likely her normal speech pattern might include a hint of a Spanish accent. Who knows, maybe the girl really *was* an actress.

"I'd give anything to hear her 'yammering' now," Shirley said wistfully. "Her funeral's Monday afternoon, at St. Luke's. We have to wait for the coroner's office to—to—" Her voice broke and she began to weep.

"It's okay," I said, putting my hand over her rougher one. I knew it wouldn't be, however. Tiffany had probably been more than a daughter to this poor woman. My guess was she'd also represented Shirley's fantasies of a better life for herself. And now, barely out of her teens, Tiffany was dead.

When Shirley regained control, I took a deep breath and broached the subject I'd come to discuss. "Did Tiffany tell you she had a part in a movie that was about to be shot?"

Shirley nodded. "Sure, the one over in Big Sur. She was on her way there when she stopped home to see her dad and me." She knotted her fingers together and took a big breath. "It—it was her big break, her chance to be noticed in Hollywood."

"Do you know the name of the movie?"

Shirley blinked a couple of times. "*Night Wind*, she said. Tiffany's new agent got her the part."

Now we were getting somewhere, I thought. "This new agent. Do you know his name?"

"Why? Is there something wrong?"

I caught the note of panic in Shirley's voice and sought to quell it. There was no point in making this poor grieving mother any more distressed, at least not until I knew for certain that her daughter's death was no accident. "No, no, nothing's wrong. I just thought I'd like to talk to him, or her. Get a little information for the *Star*."

"You're writing about Tiffany?"

"Perhaps just a short item. We like to take notice whenever somebody in our industry—one of our own—dies."

"I—I think Tiffany would have liked that," Shirley said, "being considered part of the movie industry."

I nodded encouragingly, feeling more and more like a con artist, the way I was manipulating this poor woman. What the hell, maybe I *would* write a short obit after all . . . unless Tiffany Novotny's death turned into the much bigger story I was beginning to suspect it would, of course. "Do you know the name of her new agent?" I asked again.

Shirley chewed her lip for a moment, then shook her head. "She might have said, I just don't know. Wouldn't have meant anything to me, anyway—I don't know the important movie names—so I guess I didn't pay that much attention."

"Does the name Troy Kellerman mean anything to you?"

"No. Should it?"

"Not really. He's just a young agent Tiffany met recently. I thought maybe he was the one she'd signed on with." I had no real reason to suspect Troy, except that he worked at a talent agency and I'd seen Tiffany trying to flirt with him at Shane's funeral.

"Could be. Can't you just ask him?"

"Sure, good idea. When did your daughter leave here to go to the movie location?"

"Wednesday, about noon."

"And the accident was the same night."

"Uh-huh. She had to be on the set early Thursday morning, so they wanted her to stay overnight, be in makeup by seven in the morning."

"Know where the movie company was staying?"

"One of the motels in Carmel, I think. Isn't much of anywhere to stay in Big Sur."

After last night, I could confirm that fact from personal experience. "But you don't know which motel?"

"Sorry. All Tiffany said was she'd be home again over the weekend if she got a day off, and she'd have her cell phone with her, if we needed to reach her."

Except that cell phones don't work in Big Sur, but perhaps Tiffany didn't know that.

Another tear rolled down Shirley's cheek. "I—I guess I sound like a bad mother, like I should know these things, but Tiffany was all grown up, she had her own life. I didn't want to be a meddler."

"I'm sure you were a wonderful mother," I said, using my most sincere voice. "Tiffany was lucky to have you."

"Will—will you be at her funeral?"

"I'm really sorry. I'd like to, but I have to be back at work in L.A. on Monday morning," I said, relieved to have an acceptable excuse. Two funerals so close together, both for twenty-somethings, was more than I could stomach.

"You'll send me a copy of whatever you write about Tiffany, won't you?"

"Of course." How could I say no? Now I'd have to write something. I took down Tiffany's information—her date and place of birth, plus a few human interest details about her short life—made sure I had the Novotny family's correct mailing address, and made my excuses. As I drove away past the dark-skinned men, still laboring in the fields, I couldn't help but understand Tiffany Novotny a bit better. If she hadn't entered and won that first beauty contest, if she hadn't had an aunt and uncle in Los Angeles who let her live with them while she pursued her dream of stardom, she might well have ended up reliving her mother's life.

Yet if she hadn't come to L.A., if she hadn't tried to push her way into the movie business, I wondered, would she still be alive?

7

"Nothing at the scene to indicate foul play, not that I saw. Just another tourist driving too fast for the highway." I'd tracked down Ned Harmon, the highway patrolman who'd handled the investigation of Tiffany's accident. Lucky for me, he was working the night shift again tonight and the CHP dispatcher was willing to give me the name of the Monterey diner where he habitually ate supper. Now he and I were sitting across from each other at a corner table. I was nursing a cup of coffee while Harmon wolfed down two cheeseburgers, a plate of fries, and a chocolate shake. His portly, middle-aged physique advertised that he ate this way frequently.

"There weren't any skid marks on the road where her car went off," I said. "I looked."

"She probably fell asleep at the wheel. Happens all the time."

"Could be, but there are a few other things here that don't add up." I told him about Tiffany's movie job that didn't exist, as well as my suspicions about Shane King's death.

"So you're trying to tell me this crash wasn't an accident?" Harmon said, wiping a blob of ketchup from his chin.

"I'm saying it's definitely possible it wasn't an accident, and that somebody should investigate it to be certain."

He grabbed a thick French fry and twirled it in his fingers before crumpling the whole thing into his mouth. "Girl could've committed suicide, I suppose," he said, still chewing. "No real way to tell whether folks go off these cliffs by accident or on purpose, come right down to it. Unless they leave some sort of note behind, of course. Suicides don't usually leave skid marks."

Why were cops so quick to chalk up a violent death to suicide instead of murder? First Tracy Lewis had made that assumption about Shane, and now this guy from the CHP was ready to believe Tiffany had killed herself. Maybe they just didn't want to work too hard.

"I'm not suggesting suicide," I told him as he started on his second burger. "Tiffany had no reason to kill her—"

"Hey, you told me her boyfriend just OD'd. She had to be pretty distraught."

"Like I also told you, I think Shane King might have been murdered, too. Besides, Tiffany Novotny didn't strike me as all that attached to the guy."

"So maybe the girl hid her feelings, didn't want her folks to know she was planning to kill herself."

I sighed. What Harmon was saying was possible, of course, but suicide clashed with my strong impression of Tiffany's self-centered personality. From my observation, the girl really didn't seem to give a damn about Shane and, even if she did care for him at some level, her hoped-for career seemed far more important to her than he was. "I don't buy that," I said. "I believe somebody lured her out of town with the promise of a phony acting job, then murdered her."

"Yeah? Who? And why?"

"I don't know who. Isn't that the job of the police, to find out?"

Harmon took a swig of his drink, leaving him with an ice cream mustache, and shook his head. "You reporters," he said, rolling his eyes, "always looking to make something into a sensational story."

"If you don't believe she could have been murdered, explain why somebody'd hire Tiffany to star in a movie that doesn't exist and lure her all the way up here. Hardly sounds like an innocent prank to me."

"What proof you got anybody hired her to do anything?"

"She told her aunt and uncle down in L.A. about it, plus her parents up here. She was very excited about having this chance to play a big role in a movie."

"Listen to yourself, Ms.—what did you say your name was?"

"Collins, Quinn Collins of the *Hollywood Star*." I pulled out one of my cards and slid it across the table.

"Ms. Collins. So your only proof is the girl told people she got hired to act in this bogus movie. Maybe she told them that so she'd have an excuse to come up here, see her folks one last time, then drive her car off that cliff. That ever occur to you?"

"Maybe," I conceded. "But tell me this, is the coroner examining her body for signs of foul play?"

"Sure, but don't hold your breath. A person takes a dive like that, the body's gonna be pretty beat up. Now if she was shot, if there's a bullet in her body, or if maybe her throat was slashed, that's gonna show up. If she was dead before she went off that cliff, the ME ought to be able to tell."

"What about drugs? What if she was drugged before the crash?"

"ME always does a tox screen, to see if the driver was under the influence."

My spirits began to brighten a bit. Shane was killed by drugs. Maybe Tiffany was, too. "When can I get those results?"

Harmon held up a greasy hand in protest. "Hey you can't—"

"Public record," I reminded him. "I'm entitled to see that report."

He backed down quickly. "Takes a few days. Alcohol test is pretty quick—they should know that much by now—but anything more complicated, probably not until sometime next week."

"Okay, then, guess I'll have to wait." I took down the Monterey County coroner's name and phone number. It wasn't much, but maybe my trip north would yield some small result after all. "Thanks for your help," I said, plopping two dollars on the table to pay for my coffee.

"Yeah, right."

As I reached the door, Ned Harmon was draining the last of his chocolate shake and signaling the waitress. I wondered whether his summons was for his check or some dessert. Either way, my own appetite was now history.

I spent the night in a local motel and headed back to L.A. in the morning, right after breakfast, taking the faster route south on 101 from Salinas. As I drove past the turnoff for the Novotny farm, I couldn't help but think once more about poor Shirley Novotny, mourning her only child while she waited for the coroner to release that child's battered body for burial. Maybe I'd made the right choice, never having kids of my own—at least I'd never have to bury one of them.

Traffic was light until I reached Santa Barbara, where I began to hit the Sunday afternoon rush back to the city. Even so, I made it home before four o'clock.

Uncle Teddy was out when I arrived and, after I'd unpacked my small suitcase, I found my guesthouse too quiet.

For some reason I couldn't quite put my finger on, I felt restless and lonely. At least I could use this time to start writing Tiffany's obituary, I decided. That would give me another hour at work tomorrow, and I was already nearly a day behind on this week's publication schedule, having split for the Central Coast on Friday.

I roughed out the obit at home, then decided to go into the office, where I'd left my file containing Tiffany's composite photo. I selected the shot that offered the most flattering view of the young woman's pretty face, then cropped it so the fact she was wearing a bathing suit wouldn't be evident in print.

It was peaceful here in the office, and somehow I didn't feel as lonely as I did at home. Maybe it was because nobody else was supposed to be at work late on a Sunday afternoon, while my being alone at home simply underlined just how dependent I'd become on my elderly uncle for basic companionship. I resolved to do something about my pathetic social life.

I took out a piece of paper and made a few notes about the two deaths I'd been investigating, to stretch the meaning of the term investigate. My notes took the form of unanswered questions:

"Shane died from an overdose," I wrote. "Did he lie to Peter and Tiffany about being a user?

"Tiffany's movie, *Night Wind*—did she really believe it existed or did she lie?

"Did Tiffany really have a new agent, or did she lie about that, too? If she was telling the truth, who was her agent?" I added a note to myself to call the Lance Edelson Agency in the morning and find out whether she'd been added to its client list. If not, I could probably forget about my suspicion that Troy Kellerman was somehow connected to Tiffany's death.

"Were Shane and Tiffany murdered?" I added to my list, along with, "Who would want them dead?" and "Why?"

There was one more thing I could do while I had the office to myself, I decided after compiling my list. I checked back issues of the *Star* over the past ten years for mentions of every name I could think of that could be connected to this sad series of events: Shane, Peter, Rhett, and Veronica King, Parker and Troy Kellerman.

I quickly located a series of short articles chronicling Peter's descending career and couldn't help feeling sad as I read them. He'd had such promise but, like so many Hollywood players, it had all gone up in smoke. There were always reasons, but not necessarily ones you could easily pinpoint. Maybe Peter had crossed the wrong people, or failed to suck up to the right people. Or perhaps he'd simply picked the wrong properties to direct. Once a director had a failure or two under his belt, the studio heads didn't want to take another chance. It was also possible his depression over losing his older son had made him just give up. All I could tell from this series of stories was that Peter was now officially a has-been.

Hollywood has never been kind to has-beens.

We'd run a mention of Shane King's being hired at Calistoga Studios, and I found numerous articles about Parker Kellerman's wheeling and dealing in the industry. But there was nothing here to shed any light on why two young people were dead.

Next, I logged onto the *L.A. Times* website and did the same kind of search through its back issues.

Veronica's last marriage was noted, and Rhett's suicide rated a brief mention in one of the gossip columns, largely because his father still had been a Hollywood player at the time it happened.

I found Veronica King's name several times in the social columns, as well as Parker Kellerman's.

The elder Kellerman also had a drunk driving arrest reported in ninety-four. He'd been caught driving erratically along Sunset Boulevard in Brentwood. And the real estate section noted the sale of the Kellermans' Pacific Palisades house to a movie star in ninety-six for "in excess of its three-million-dollar asking price."

The *Times*' only mention of Troy Kellerman was in the final paragraphs of an article about the slaying of Palisades High School student Lauren Hartley. Rhett King was mentioned in the same story, as were several other Pali High students. As I read the details off the computer screen, I realized that this was the murder Peter had told me about, the event he believed had spurred Rhett's downward slide into heavier and heavier drug use, ultimately ending in his suicide.

Basically, the article told the same story Peter had related to me when we had lunch at Ocean Avenue Seafood. A group of Pali High students had been partying at the beach. Between the lines, I read that the Pali kids had been drinking and probably using drugs as well, so they were undoubtedly far less than coherent. At some point during the night, they noticed Lauren was missing and went looking for her.

Her body was found lying at the base of a lifeguard station the next morning. She'd been sexually assaulted and strangled.

When the police finally were called, the party-goers reported having seen a group of Latinos at the beach earlier in the evening. One of the Latinos was their classmate, Luis

Alvarez. The Alvarez youth was among those students voluntarily bused to Pali from a poorer section of L.A. for purposes of racial integration. None of the more affluent students recognized anyone else in the other group.

I searched for additional stories about the murder and found quite a few, undoubtedly because Lauren had been a rich white girl from a classy part of town. If she'd been a poor minority, raped and murdered in Watts or East L.A., her demise wouldn't have rated a line in the *Times* or any other big newspaper. Such a brutal crime in Pacific Palisades, however, was considered genuine news.

I printed out all of the *Times*' stories about the Hartley girl's murder and skimmed them briefly. Besides Rhett King and Troy Kellerman, other Pali students mentioned as being at the ill-fated party included Stevenson Brooks, Joseph Taliaferro, and Julia Jackson. One article even included what looked like a small yearbook photo of each one. All of them told the same story about seeing the Latinos hanging around on the beach and exchanging a few words with them, then sometime later in the evening noticing that Lauren was missing. The girl had gone off on her own, saying she was going to the ladies' room, and no one noticed for some time that she'd never returned. Rather than call the police right away, they decided to look for her themselves, figuring that would be faster.

I suspected the real reason the kids didn't call the police as soon as they realized the girl was gone was that they'd wanted to sober up before facing the authorities. And, since their parents were all rich and powerful people in this town, the cops wouldn't have hassled them too much on that score.

Peter's conclusion that waiting to call the cops was what had haunted Rhett afterward—if he'd simply called for help as soon as Lauren's absence was noticed, would she still be alive?—seemed logical to me. There seemed to be no question that Rhett had stayed at the party the entire night—all his friends vouched for his presence—so the cops never considered him a suspect in Lauren's death. Still, I could see how he, and perhaps the others as well, might feel somewhat responsible—they'd all failed to keep Lauren safe.

The most recent articles chronicled the arrest and ultimate plea bargain of Luis Alvarez for the second-degree murder of Lauren Hartley. The only thing that seemed a bit odd was that, despite confessing his own guilt, young Alvarez had refused to name any of his companions. He stuck to the claim that he'd been alone on the beach that night. Misplaced loyalty to his friends, I figured, or more likely, fear. He might well have been afraid for his life if he ratted out his accomplices, and doing so wouldn't necessarily have lessened the twenty-five-year-to-life sentence he'd received. For all I knew, his fellow rapists had been gang members with strong connections inside the prison system.

I took my printouts and put them together into a new file folder, labeled the folder "Shane King," and slid it into a drawer.

I glanced at the clock. It was now after six. With any luck, Uncle Teddy would be home cooking one of his marvelous dinners. Suddenly I remembered I'd eaten nothing more than today's breakfast during the past twenty-eight hours, and I was starving.

Maybe, too, I thought, if I spent the evening having a good meal and some stimulating conversation, I could get the pictures of all these dead young people out of my mind.

Reinventing my social life could wait for another day.

* * * * *

When I got home, Uncle Teddy was sipping a glass of sauvignon blanc with our neighbor, Sylvia St. Clair.

"Ah, just in time, sweetheart," he said, giving me as big a hug as if I'd been away for a month. "I'm marinating the salmon and the wild rice pilaf is in the oven. You're definitely joining us, aren't you?"

My growling stomach testified that I had absolutely no intention of refusing.

"Nothing like Teddy's salmon," Sylvia told me, sighing deeply. "Simply melts in your mouth, and that sesame butter sauce he puts on it is to *die* for . . ." She continued to applaud my uncle's culinary skills as though I hadn't been eating his fabulous meals since I was a toddler. Sometimes, I must admit, I hold Teddy's skills in the kitchen responsible for my expanding waistline. His exceptional talent is probably also the main reason I never bothered to learn to cook decently myself. Why would I need to when I lived with a man who could have been a professional chef?

Sylvia, who was a few years older than Teddy, had been a starlet many years ago, but her real career had been marriage. Now well into her seventies, she'd had her face lifted and tucked at least three times that I knew about, had dyed her hair an unlikely shade of red, and had taken to wearing flowing, diaphanous gowns to disguise her spreading girth. Tonight, she was wearing a bright crimson creation almost the same shade as her hair. As she flitted about the kitchen, refilling wine glasses, I couldn't help being reminded of a flickering flame.

Sylvia was a woman completely devoted to gossip, particularly about the movie industry, and since his beloved Artie's death, she'd become Teddy's most frequent companion. She was a unique character and I was immensely fond of her. As we sipped our wine, she regaled us with the latest rumors about which actress would land the next coveted role opposite Brad Pitt, whether Meg Ryan's brief affair with Russell Crowe would impact her career, and the current state of Michael J. Fox's health.

When I brought up agent Lance Edelson's name at dinner half an hour later, Sylvia had plenty to contribute as well, giving me a complete chronicle of Edelson's rise to the higher echelons of one of the town's biggest talent agencies, followed by his breaking away to start the Lance Edelson Talent Agency.

"I was represented by Lance myself, for a couple of years back in the seventies," she added. "I was semi-retired by then, of course, and Lance was just starting out in the business. Unlike some of his competition—" She made a sour face, "—he was a real sweetie, never treated me like a tiresome old broad, the way some of those young punk agents did. He got me small parts on a few sitcoms and in one or two TV movies. I played Elizabeth Montgomery's sister in one, I remember, and I played a secretary on a movie of the week, I think with that guy from Mannix . . . what the hell's his name?" She slapped a hand against her forehead, making the four heavy gold bracelets circling her wrist jangle. "Lord, my memory just gets worse and worse."

"Mike Connors," I prompted.

"Of course, Quinnie, Mike Connors, that's the fellow. How quick we forget, right?"

I nodded.

"Anyway," she continued, "this was when I was between husbands." That had been a fairly common state for Sylvia. "I was divorcing Graham—remember, he was the SOB who filed bankruptcy after hiding all his money in Swiss banks, practically left me living on the street—and before I married dear old Franklin. So I was, shall we say, sorely in need of a little pocket change?" She raised her penciled-on eyebrows and shook her head as if to ask how she could have gotten herself into that kind of mess—a situation where she actually had to support herself, however briefly.

"Well, it was wonderful luck you had Lance Edelson on your side when you needed him," I replied, trying to keep a smirk off my face. When Franklin, Sylvia's fifth and final husband, died, he left her his millions, guaranteeing she'd never find herself in need of pocket change again. She promptly swore off marriage, and has never been happier.

"Damn right it was lucky, Quinnie, and I never forgot Lance for it, either. I send him one of Teddy's fabulous rum-soaked Christmas cakes every year, and he never fails to send me a personal note of thanks."

I couldn't help giggling, although I tried my best to hide my mirth behind my napkin. To this day, Sylvia still manages to get men to give her gifts, even gay men. She expects their attention and somehow she always seems to get it. She wasn't the least bit embarrassed to admit she'd been having Uncle Teddy bake the Christmas treats she undoubtedly was passing off as her own creations, either.

"So I'll call Edelson tomorrow morning and ask about Tiffany Novotny," I said, scooping up the last of my wild rice pilaf. "This really is superb, Teddy. You've outdone yourself again."

"Lance or his people give you any trouble, you just call me," Sylvia said, helping herself to a third portion of fresh asparagus. "What did you put in this hollandaise?" she asked, turning to Teddy. "It's positively heavenly."

He told her.

"Why would Edelson give me trouble?" I asked, directing the conversation back to my problem. "It's an easy enough question, isn't it? 'Was Tiffany Novotny on your client list?' "

"Could be she was a pocket client, like I was."

"What do you mean, pocket client?" I wasn't familiar with the term.

"If he still operates like he did in the old days, Lance sometimes takes on people without signing a formal contract, particularly those who want only occasional work, like I did, or newcomers he might not be able to sell. Called us his pocket clients. I'm just thinking, if this girl was new to the business, he might have agreed to work with her for a only brief time and, if she didn't click at any of the auditions he got her, he'd dump her."

"He could do that anyway, under the standard SAG contract." The Screen Actors Guild allows either an agent or a client to terminate their relationship if the actor gets no paying jobs after a specified period of time.

"But then the failure becomes public and, in this town, people gossip. The actor's reputation suffers, and so does the agent's." Sylvia speared her last piece of fish. "Just offering to make a call for you, dear, in case Lance's secretary claims she never heard of this girl. Might be reasons they wouldn't want their representation of a dead young actress publicized in this week's *Star*, right?"

I had to admit she had a valid point. It was logical that the Edelson Agency would blow me off rather than admit anything less than a fully contractual relationship with Tiffany Novotny. I now could see that I'd probably have only one shot at asking the questions I wanted to ask, too.

"Tell you what, Sylvia. If you don't mind, could you ask Lance to see me, as a personal favor? Don't tell him what it's about—you don't know what I want, but we're friends and you promised me, whatever. Just ask him to give me a few minutes as soon as possible." I began to realize that, if I told Edelson's staff ahead of time what this was about and tried to make my own appointment, they'd just put me off. If I even managed to see the agency chief at all, it would be three or four weeks from now, and it wouldn't do to ask my questions over the phone. I wanted to see Lance Edelson's and Troy Kellerman's faces when they answered.

"Sure, Quinnie, glad to help out," Sylvia said. "I'll call dear Lance first thing in the morning." She turned to my uncle. "I saw some of your lovely creme brulee in the fridge, didn't I, Teddy?" she asked in a coquettish voice.

I tried to summon enough courage to refuse dessert, knowing full well I'd regret every calorie in the morning, but I failed miserably. Instead, as I enjoyed the creamy custard dissolving on my tongue, I simply told myself I'd swim an extra ten laps before breakfast.

Sylvia was as good as her word. I spent the morning in the office, rewriting a few news releases for the next edition and assigning Lucy a few research tasks. By one o'clock, I was at Lance Edelson's office on the twenty-eighth floor of a Century City office tower. His buxom young red-haired secretary ushered me into his private suite without even making me wait, which is standard Hollywood practice. Sylvia must have had some real clout with this guy.

Edelson didn't rise from his executive's chair when I entered the room, simply indicated that I should choose one of the matching pale gray leather chairs facing his massive kidney-shaped teak desk.

"Thanks for seeing me on such short notice," I said, leaning across the desk to shake the agent's hand before sitting down. He was probably in his mid-fifties, buffed up, and fashionably tanned. He wore his light brown hair in a brush cut I suspected had been helped along by fairly recent hair plug surgery.

"I had a few minutes free and it's hard to say no to Sylvia," he told me with a wry smile. "Always was a very determined woman."

"Don't I know it."

"So what's this about?" Obviously Edelson didn't intend to waste time making small talk with a reporter from the *Star.*

"I'm researching a story about a young actress I believe was one of your new clients." If in doubt, act like you already have the information and you're simply seeking confirmation, that's my motto. "Tiffany Novotny."

The crease between Edelson's eyebrows deepened. "Tiffany Novotny? I don't think she was on our client list, but the name sounds vaguely familiar."

"Could you check to be sure?"

He pressed a button on his intercom and spoke into it. "Suzie, check the computer and see if we've ever represented an actress named Tiffany Novotny, will you?" He released the button and turned back to me. "If she is one of our clients, I'm sure I'd have suggested she change that name," he said, making a face like he smelled something bad.

"Tiffany or Novotny?"

Rolling his eyes, he replied, "Both."

The intercom buzzed and Edelson pushed another of its buttons.

"No Tiffany Novotny on our list of clients, either currently or in the past," his secretary reported.

"Thanks, Suzie."

"Maybe Tiffany was one of your pocket clients," I suggested, watching the agent's demeanor.

Edelson paused a beat before answering. He tented his fingers on his pristine desktop. "I don't know what you mean, 'pocket client,' " he said, straight-faced.

"Really. Off the books, represented temporarily without a signed SAG contract, the way you helped Sylvia St. Clair with those TV deals."

He shook his head. "Sylvia was a long time ago, with another agency. Tiffany Novotny's definitely not one of ours. Now, if you don't mind, I'm—"

"Tiffany's dead," I told him.

"Dead?" Recognition swept over his suntanned face. "So that's why that name is familiar. I must have heard something on the news about her being killed. Can't remember any details, though."

"Her car went off a cliff in Big Sur. She was in it."

"And what makes you think she had any connection to the Edelson Agency?"

"Right before she died, she told her family she'd landed a new agent, and she's an acquaintance of your assistant, Troy Kellerman. I simply added two and two and—"

"Came up with thirty-seven."

"Hey, maybe I'm way off base here, Mr. Edelson, but let me ask you one more thing—was Troy in the office last Wednesday?"

"Why?"

"I'm curious, and that information could let me put a hunch to rest. If I knew for sure, I wouldn't have to include anything about your agency in my story."

Edelson thought for a moment. "Wednesday." He consulted his electronic day planner. "Troy definitely was here all day. We signed a top TV director that afternoon, and there was a great deal of paperwork necessary to get his network residuals straightened out. Everything had to be completed before our contract could be finalized, and that sort of thing's part of Troy's responsibilities."

"And he was here on Thursday as well?"

Edelson pushed back his chair and, noticing the look on his face, I wondered for an instant if he intended to grab me and throw me out of his office physically. "Troy was not only in the office on Thursday, he accompanied one of our young female clients to a screening Wednesday night. I can vouch for that personally. I was there, and I saw them."

"Thanks," I said, standing up. Maybe my hunch had been wrong about Troy Kellerman. Just because Tiffany had been hanging on him at Shane's funeral and he worked for a talent agency didn't mean he'd killed her. And why would he? I didn't even *have* a hunch about that.

"So what's all this about, anyway?" Edelson demanded before I could leave. "You act like you're investigating a murder or something."

"Thanks for your time," I said, thrusting out my hand. The agent shook it with markedly less enthusiasm than he had upon my arrival. "Just making sure there's nothing suspicious about the young actress' death, that's all." I quickly let myself out of his office, pulling the door shut behind me.

Troy Kellerman was leaning over Edelson's secretary, apparently peering down her cleavage, when I emerged into the reception area. His thick thatch of dark hair fell into his eyes as he whispered something in Suzie's ear. As I approached, he stopped talking and glanced up. I thought I caught a fleeting look of rage on his face before he managed to replace it with the kind of bland facade so many of today's young people seem to have mastered.

"Hello, Troy," I said, thrusting out my hand. "Remember me?" I wondered if he'd been listening on Suzie's intercom.

His hand was damp and his handshake no more than a brief, unenthusiastic squeeze. "Ms. Connell, right?"

"Collins. Quinn Collins. We met at Shane King's funeral."

"Right. Now I remember." He didn't ask me what I was doing there. I suspected he already knew and was angry as hell about it.

Whether he'd done anything wrong or not, I realized, I'd possibly just jeopardized his job by talking to his boss about him. He had every right to resent me. Unless, of course, he really did have something to do with Tiffany's death, in which case his self-protective instincts were probably kicking in right about now.

"Got a minute?" I asked.

He glanced at his watch, unsmiling. "No more than two. I've got work to do." He led me into his office and closed the door behind us. His digs were nearly small enough to fit inside the coat closet in Edelson's palatial suite.

"What are you on my case for? I hardly even knew that girl," he demanded, standing in front of his desk, his arms folded across his chest.

So he had been eavesdropping, or at least he knew Suzie had searched the agency's database for Tiffany's name. "When I saw you two together, Tiffany certainly seemed interested in getting to know you better," I said.

"So? Lots of young actresses are like that. Long as I work for Lance, I've got power in this town. Unless you just managed to completely fuck it up for me."

"Ever heard of a movie called *Night Wind*, Troy?"

"Nope." He stroked the strange little patch of whiskers that sprouted just below his lower lip. To me, it looked more like he'd drooled chocolate onto his chin than some new fashion. Then again, maybe I was getting too old to appreciate the latest youthful fad in facial hair.

"Tiffany thought she'd been hired to play a part in *Night Wind*," I explained, "told everybody her new agent got her a starring role. Only problem is, far as I can tell, no movie named *Night Wind* exists, and her family doesn't even know the name of her new agent. That, coupled with the fact she's dead, makes me a touch suspicious. Must be my journalistic training."

"Look," Troy said, his volume dropping a notch, "I'm sorry she's dead, I really am, but the girl was nothing but a whore. *Night Wind* is probably some porno picture she got herself involved in, something being shot off the books somewhere in Van Nuys. You ask me, Shane King was an idiot to take up with a slut like that in the first place. Always did think with his goddamn dick."

"And you know Tiffany was a whore exactly *how?*"

Troy finally had the grace to color slightly. "Everybody knew it. I mean, look at the way she acted at Shane's funeral. Coming on to me like that. Shit, the guy she's supposedly in love with's not even cold and she's hitting on his friends. Why would I want to get involved with a tease like that?"

"Know any of Shane's other friends who might have standards a little bit lower than yours?"

Troy opened his office door again. "You came to the wrong place," he told me with a sneer.

I quickly calculated my options and decided it was time to leave.

"Got those addresses and phone numbers you asked for," Lucy said as I entered the *Star*'s reception area. She thrust a piece of paper at me. "These three aren't listed in the phone books, but then I remembered my next door neighbor's sister is a counselor at Pali Hi. Name's Hannah Ruiz." She smiled broadly. "We got lucky, Quinn—Hannah's been keeping an updated address list for most of the Pali grads, at least the ones still in the L.A. area. She got this off her alumni list and she actually even still remembers these kids."

"Great work, Lucy," I told her, quickly seeing that she'd supplied the current contact information I'd requested for Stevenson Brooks, Joseph Taliaferro, and Julia Jackson, the Palisades High School students who'd been partying at the beach on the night Lauren Hartley was murdered. There was probably no connection between them and either Shane King or Tiffany Novotny, but it couldn't hurt to know how to reach them, just in case. "This counselor must have a helluva memory," I said. "It's been almost ten years since these kids graduated."

Lucy sipped her coffee, then looked up at me guiltily. "Want a cup? I can make another pot, no trouble."

I shook my head. "Thanks, but I've already had my caffeine fix for the day."

"Seemed amazing to me, too, that she'd remember these kids after all this time, so I asked her about it. Hannah admits she doesn't remember everybody—Pali's graduated thousands since these three, and nobody could remember all of them. Says she only remembers the ones who stand out, like some of her grads who went on to act on TV and the boy who became a rock star. Then there are the celebrities' kids, that sort of thing, plus one girl who's now one of the governor's aides in Sacramento."

"Did she say what made Brooks, Taliaferro and Jackson stand out in her mind?"

Lucy nodded. "Their connection to that girl who was raped and murdered."

"Lauren Hartley."

"Right, that's her name, Lauren. Hannah's been a counselor at Pali for almost twenty years, and she told me there've been several students who died during her tenure. One was shot by a deranged homeless man. One was blown up by a pipe bomb he was building in his garage. Then there were a handful of gang murders—students bused in from poorer parts of L.A.—and eleven suicides. She remembers all of them vividly. When a teenager dies, I guess it's not something you easily forget."

I nodded, thinking that counselor Hannah Ruiz could be a valuable source if there turned out to be any connection between these Pali grads and my research on Shane and Tiffany.

"What about Shane King? She remember him?"

"Didn't think to ask, but she did mention Rhett King. He didn't die until a year or two after he graduated, but Hannah heard about it and it definitely made a lasting impression on her. Figured at first it might've been suicide. Sounds like suicides were hardest on her, like she felt it was her job to know those kids were depressed and stop them from destroying themselves. My guess is she considers them her personal failures."

"I can see how she might feel that way." I looked at the paper Lucy had typed and saw some notes about what Jackson and Taliaferro were doing these days. The space after Brooks' name, however, was blank. "I guess Hannah Ruiz doesn't know where Stevenson Brooks works now," I said.

"Far as she knows, he's unemployed, being supported by his wealthy father. He has two younger sisters who've been through Pali since Parker graduated, so she's been able to keep up with his life fairly well. Seems he's been through at least two drug rehabs and has lost half a dozen jobs his dad got for him. Basically, he's not doing at all well."

"Drug rehabs, huh?" Suddenly my interest was piqued. I glanced over at Harry's closed office door. "Harry in?" I asked.

"Still at lunch," Lucy told me, glancing at the clock on the wall. "He's trying to sell ABC on running a series of full-page ads congratulating their Emmy nominees, the sort of thing the studios do for the Oscars."

"Good," I said, grabbing my purse and briefcase off the chair where I'd dumped them. "If he wants to know where I am, tell him I'm still taking that personal time off he forced upon me."

I started out the door, then stopped myself. "Hey, Lucy," I said, "ever think you're wasting your talents as a secretary? You should be a reporter."

"Come on," she said, shaking her head. "I love my job and I'm too shy to go out interviewing people the way you do. Besides, I'm much too old to learn new tricks now."

"Your decision. Just want you to know you did real good work today." As I closed the door, I saw that Lucy was beaming with satisfaction. I made a mental note to buy her flowers or take her to lunch. Soon.

Stevenson Brooks' apartment was on Bundy Drive in Brentwood, just about three blocks north of the spot where Nicole Brown Simpson and Ronald Goldman were slashed to death. Not that I had reason to suspect young Stevenson of that particular crime, even if O.J. was still looking for his ex-wife's "real killer."

I found curbside parking two doors down and rang his

doorbell. I figured Brooks' being unemployed might well mean he'd be home during the daytime and roaming the streets at night. But maybe I was wrong. There was no answer.

I rang again, then a third time, before a static-muddled voice finally came through the intercom mounted at the side of the door. "Whadya want?" The speaker didn't sound happy.

"I've got something here for Stevenson Brooks," I replied. Questions, to be more specific.

"Hold on."

It was nearly five minutes before the door was opened by a red-eyed man in a soiled bathrobe. I stared openly, trying to reconcile this guy with the photo of Stevenson Brooks in the *Times*, the shot of the dark-haired teenage boy with the cocky grin. The wasted man in the doorway was much thinner, unshaven, long-haired, foul-breathed, and definitely not grinning. He also looked at least fifteen or twenty years older than the student who'd partied on the beach the night a girl died, but maybe that was just hard living taking its toll.

"Stevenson Brooks?" I asked tentatively.

"You found me. If you're selling something, I don't want any." Still no grin.

"I'm not selling anything. I'm Quinn Collins, of the *Hollywood Star*. I'd like to talk to you about Shane King."

There was a long pause as Brooks' bloodshot eyes darted upward, then stared over my shoulder. Searching for any cops I might have brought with me? Apparently he didn't spot any. "Who?" he said eventually.

"Shane King. Your old friend Rhett's younger brother."

"Shane and Rhett are dead. I don't know jack." He started to close the door.

I stuck my foot in it.

"Look, Stevenson—Steve, I'm not here to hassle you. I know you've had your problems with drugs and all, but I'm not here to bust you. I'm a reporter, not a narc. I just thought—" I struggled to find something I could tell him other than the truth—that as soon as I'd learned about his history with drugs, I'd figured he might know who bought the heroin that killed Shane. "I already talked with Troy Kellerman," I said.

The pressure of the door on my foot lessened as Stevenson took half a step backward.

"Troy? Why? What'd *he* say?" Did I detect a leap of fear in the man's eyes or was it simply irritation over being wakened in the middle of the afternoon by a pushy blonde?

"Let's go inside," I said, pushing against the door. "You don't really want your neighbors overhearing us, do you?"

Stevenson gripped the ties of his robe, pulled them tighter around his scrawny waist, and stepped aside. The inside of his place smelled as bad as he did. There were food-encrusted dishes on the coffee table and the countertop between the living room and kitchen, and dirty clothes were strewn all over the furniture and floor. An unmade single bed occupied an alcove off the living room. This place looked like the room of a teenager whose mother had refused to clean up after him, ever again. I looked around, but didn't see a clean spot to sit down. My host made no move to clear a surface for me, so I remained standing.

"What'd Troy tell you?" Stevenson demanded again.

"He and I couldn't really come to a conclusion about whether Shane was a drug user before he OD'd that day," I improvised. "We thought you might know, Steve."

He seemed relieved. "I—I heard he was." Slouching against the wall, he picked at a spot on his cheek with a dirty fingernail.

"From where?"

"Huh?"

"Where did you hear that Shane was a user? Who told you that?"

Again he avoided making eye contact. "Used to see him at—at some of the clubs I like. He was pretty wasted."

"Are you sure he was high, or could he just have had too much to drink?"

Stevenson shrugged his shoulders. Even with the robe covering them, they looked bony. "Booze, H, coke, ecstasy, whatever he could get. Who knows. Just like his big brother. Couple of major assholes, you want my opinion."

"Why do you think that?"

"What?" The fingers picking at Stevenson's face began to tremble slightly.

"That Rhett and Shane were a couple of assholes."

"Killed themselves, right? If that's not pretty fucked-up, what is?"

"So you think Shane's death was suicide? What makes you believe that, Steve? Was he depressed?"

Looking increasingly exhausted, he shook his shaggy head and closed his eyes for a moment, then seemed to snap himself awake again. "Look, lady, I don't know jack shit about Shane King, okay? He was just my old buddy's screwed-up kid brother is all—I hardly knew him. Now, I was up all night and I'm going back to bed." He reopened the front door, wincing as a trapezoid of bright afternoon sunlight hit his eyes. He jerked aside, looking relieved to be back in the shadows again.

This was the third time today I'd been thrown out of an

interview. I was beginning to think I might break my personal record.

I left without bothering to shake Stevenson Brooks' hand.

I spent the rest of the afternoon back at the office, making phone calls and writing a handful of stories I could research without leaving my desk.

By the time I left, I felt as tired as Stevenson Brooks had looked, but my workday was far from over. I headed home, made myself a sandwich for dinner, redid my makeup, changed into my emerald green silk cocktail dress, and headed across town to the wrap party for the latest Spielberg picture.

Uncle Teddy always goes to his bridge club meeting on Monday night, so I was on my own this time. Just as well, I figured. If the party was a dud, I could slip out without being noticed. But if I had Teddy with me, he'd manage to find some old crony to converse with until the wee hours. He always did.

It turned out the party was anything but a dud. Everybody who'd worked on the picture was there, of course, along with what seemed like half the rest of the town. There was an incredibly lavish spread of food and drink and a couple of great new bands providing entertainment. I picked up some good industry gossip, too, some of which I thought I might even be able to use in the *Star.*

Many of the informational tidbits—which star's marriage was about to break up, which director was boffing which starlet younger than his daughter—weren't really useful for the sort of articles I write. To Sylvia St. Clair's eternal disappointment, I'm not now and never will be a Hollywood gossip columnist.

Other items—particularly some knowledgeable, insider opinions on which industry guilds were prepared to strike during the coming year if their demands weren't met by the producers—were far more useful. They would give me valuable background in the near future, when the unions' contracts came up for renegotiation.

It was well after midnight before I got home. I was bone-tired and could feel a headache coming on, the result of drinking too much wine. My feet were killing me, too—whoever invented high-heeled shoes ought to be condemned to wear them twenty-four/seven for the rest of eternity, if you ask me.

I parked in my usual spot in the driveway next to the main house and, as I walked past the house, I saw Uncle Teddy's lights were off. As usual, he must have come home from his bridge club around ten. I smiled, certain he was fast asleep by now.

Relieved that none of the neighbors could see me over the six-foot fence surrounding the back of the property, I stopped a moment and slipped off my uncomfortable shoes, then walked stocking-footed along the path that led around the pool to my little guesthouse. The cool, fog-dampened concrete soothed my swollen, aching feet.

The pool light was off tonight, but I thought I spotted something pale floating on the surface of the water. Leaves that had blown in over the fence, I decided, feeling irritated that I'd have to scoop them out before I could swim my morning laps. That meant another fifteen minutes of sleep I wouldn't get, not if I was going to make it into the office on time tomorrow.

I stuck my key in the guesthouse lock and twisted, but the knob seemed to turn a bit too easily and I didn't hear the usual reassuring click. Could I have left the place unlocked? I could have sworn . . .

I opened the door, stepped inside, and snapped on the light. Tired and bleary-eyed as I was, it took a moment for the devastation to register.

My cozy little home had been completely trashed!

Torn papers and broken glass lay all over the carpeting, and somebody had poured orange juice and milk and smashed eggs on the kitchen floor. Most chilling of all, the word *BITCH* had been scrawled across the living room walls in something blood red—was it ketchup, or maybe paint?

Certainly it couldn't really be blood, although I had no doubt its color was intended to make me believe it was.

A glance at my home office in the dining room showed me my file cabinet had been overturned and emptied and my computer terminal was gone. The monitor lay on the floor, its screen bashed in.

I looked beyond the wreckage and saw that the bedroom door was closed.

My breath caught and in a flash I was wide awake and completely sober. Was whoever'd done this still here, waiting for me to enter my bedroom? As I backed out the doorway and ran back toward the main house, another, even more dreadful thought hit me.

Maybe I'd been lucky I'd stayed out so late. But Uncle Teddy'd come home hours earlier.

Those red letters on the walls flashed before my eyes as I ran along the path, my shoes still in my hand. Maybe they had been written in blood after all, I thought. And what if that pale mass I'd seen floating in the pool wasn't just a clump of dead leaves?

I began to fear the unthinkable—that my poor old uncle had interrupted the burglars. That *BITCH* had been written on my walls in *his* blood. That he was—

"Teddy! Uncle Teddy!" I screamed as I pounded on his back door with my fists. I felt utterly devastated, chilled to the bone by the fear I might never see Teddy, the dear old man who was my only family, alive again.

"Teddy!" I screamed again, tears streaming down my face. "Teddy!"

8

After what seemed an eternity, a light flashed on inside the house, the door creaked open, and I saw Uncle Teddy standing there in his old-fashioned flannel nightshirt, his face creased with sleep. I threw my arms around his slender shoulders and hugged him hard, probably scaring the poor man half to death.

"Quinn! What on earth?" he asked. "Why didn't you use your key?"

As Teddy asked me the obvious question, I realized I'd left my keys hanging from the lock on the guesthouse door. "I—I was so scared you were—" I wiped my eyes, took a deep breath, and blurted out what I'd discovered in the guesthouse.

Cool-headed and efficient as ever, Teddy pulled me inside, closed and locked his backdoor, and phoned the police. They arrived in less than ten minutes and quickly determined that nobody was hiding in my bedroom. At least not anymore.

The intruder had entered through my bedroom window, which was well hidden from public view by the high pool fence. He'd broken a pane of glass so he could reach in and unlock the window. Then he'd simply raised the sash and climbed through. He'd undoubtedly left through the front door, which was why I'd found it unlocked.

Accompanied by one of the patrol officers, Teddy switched on the pool light. I wouldn't be swimming laps again anytime soon. The pale mass floating on the surface turned out to be papers from my file cabinet. Some had already been sucked into the pool's filtration system, thoroughly clogging it. At the bottom of the pool, smashed and soaked, lay my computer terminal.

No, I didn't know what might be missing, I told the police, nor did I know who'd done this. Did burglars generally leave a house as trashed as this one, or was this a revenge crime? Or maybe the destruction was simply a ploy to make a theft appear to be vandalism. I certainly didn't know.

The fact was, I didn't really own much worth stealing—my TV and stereo system were still in the guesthouse, although now they were broken and useless, and I didn't keep any money or good jewelry in my house. What else was worth taking?

If this was sheer vandalism, I had a few hunches about people who might be less than pleased with me at the present time. I'd angered at least half a dozen with things I'd written about them in the *Star* recently, career-altering secrets I'd revealed. Not the least of them was young Pierce Ireland, the director who'd filed that big lawsuit against the paper. I'd heard some scuttlebutt at the party earlier tonight that he'd just been fired off his picture.

Then there was a lecherous assistant director, a geezer old enough to be my father, who kept trying to get me into bed; I invariably refused him. The last time he'd waylaid me on a movie set, thrown his arm around me and copped a feel, I'd told him in no uncertain terms to stop harassing me or I'd report him to the producer. His instant retort was, "You're gonna be real sorry you said that, Quinn." Was this his way of making sure I was sorry? I couldn't quite picture the AD climbing through my bedroom window, but maybe he was more agile than he looked. Come to think of it, he must have been in pretty good physical shape for his age, given the number of younger women he was rumored to have bedded.

The trashing of my home could also be the work of young Troy Kellerman, I thought, although this seemed like a pretty extreme reaction to my asking his boss a few questions. Or maybe it had some other connection to my poking into the deaths of Shane and Tiffany.

And if I was going to suspect half the people I'd talked to today, there was always Stevenson Brooks. Was this the sort of "wilding" adventure Steve and his buddies might undertake after they'd had a few hits of their latest drug of choice?

Or maybe this crime was entirely random—simply some local kids raising hell on an otherwise quiet Monday night.

I didn't share any of these thoughts with the cops. Chances were I was way off base anyway, I told myself, and why make an already tense situation even worse by siccing the police on people who might have nothing to do with this?

After I told them I didn't have a clue who might have done this to me, the cops said they'd bring in a fingerprint technician in the morning to go over the guesthouse, and they'd ask the neighbors some questions as well. Maybe somebody'd seen something. I didn't get the impression this would be a high priority for the LAPD, however. After all, nobody'd been injured or killed and, if I couldn't even tell them what was missing, my financial losses couldn't be more than a few thousand dollars. Surely my insurance policy would cover that much.

About all we could really determine about the crime right now was that the damage had to have been done before Teddy'd come home at ten-fifteen. He'd neither seen nor heard anything in his backyard. Surely, if the intruder was still there that late, my uncle would have noticed lights while the man was tearing my place apart, or at least heard splashing when my belongings were thrown into the pool.

The fact that the main house hadn't been attacked might mean I was the sole target, or it might mean nothing at all. Teddy has a fairly valuable art collection, so he installed a security alarm system in his house some years back. Every one of his windows bears a small sticker warning potential intruders of its existence. He hadn't bothered wiring his guesthouse, however, because he never expected anybody would venture inside the pool fence. Besides, he didn't keep any of his valuable works of art there. Now, he promised, he would definitely make that investment, just as soon as the place had been put back in shape well enough for me to resume living there.

As crime victims go, I tried telling myself at four o'clock, when the police finally left, I was lucky. Nobody had been hurt, and Uncle Teddy had a comfortable guest room where I could sleep. I didn't even have to find myself a motel room for the rest of the night.

I've heard people say that being robbed or burgled is as bad as being raped, but I've never bought that. Frankly, I don't think any of those people have ever been raped or they'd see the difference. I've interviewed rape victims and this wasn't nearly as bad as what they'd been subjected to. What had been taken from me were mere material possessions, and material possessions could always be replaced.

Still, I had to admit I felt invaded, unsafe, as though some part of my faith in humanity had been trashed along with my belongings.

As I lay in bed in Teddy's guestroom, listening to the ticking of the grandfather clock in the hallway, I regretted the loss of my TV and stereo, my books and clothes. But what stung most was the loss of my work—my computer, my files, the fruits of my research and imagination and best creative efforts. Perhaps I could reconstruct the raw information I'd lost, I thought, but the way I wrote each story next time would undoubtedly be at least a little different from the way I'd written it before. The same lead or turn of phrase would not occur to me a second time.

Maybe I hadn't been raped, but nothing would ever be quite the same for me again.

I dragged myself into the office an hour and a half late, having managed to find a dress and pair of shoes that weren't either destroyed or covered with raw eggs and sour milk. Luckily, I'd left my briefcase in the car, so it hadn't been touched.

I could have called in sick, I suppose, spent the day trying to make order out of chaos in the guesthouse. But I didn't really want to hang around home. Watching the police technicians adding black dust to the devastation that already existed was just too damn depressing. And, once the cops were finished with my place, Uncle Teddy would call the insurance company, then the disaster cleanup team we'd used after the earthquake. I didn't need to be there.

"Well, hello Quinn. Good morning. Sure hope we didn't interrupt your beauty sleep," Harry sniped as I walked in the door.

"You missed all the excitement," Lucy said, trying as usual to make everything nice. She hates the way Harry and I are always at each other's throats, even though neither of us ever manages to stay angry for long.

"You got that right, Lucy," Harry said.

"Had a little excitement of my own to cope with," I said, unsmiling.

"Yeah?" Harry said. "Big night at the Spielberg party, huh? Well, our excitement is just a wee bit more important than who you danced with last night—the cops just left."

I stopped in my tracks. "Cops? What cops?"

Harry began to pace the reception room nervously. "Somebody broke in here last night. Jimmied the door and tripped the silent alarm. Lucky for us, Santa Monica Security scared them off before they could do any damage."

"You mean they actually got in?"

"For two, three minutes, maybe. Our security guy was patrolling on Twentieth Street when the alarm went off. Got here fast. Minute he pulled up out front with his lights flashing, he says he saw a couple of guys light out the door and run down the street."

"What did they take?" This was too much. It had to be the same guys who'd invaded my home, unless there was some sort of gang targeting the *Star* and its employees.

Harry shrugged, holding his palms upward. "Doesn't look like they took a thing."

I glanced through the cockeyed door into my office and noticed one of my file drawers was standing wide open. "I'm sure I closed that file drawer," I said.

"Don't look at me. I didn't open it."

I headed into my office as fast as I could and bent over the cabinet, my heart in my throat again. Had more of my work been ruined? I quickly thumbed through my files, but nothing seemed to be missing or destroyed.

"Maybe this is where the crooks started," Lucy offered, "in your office."

"Probably has something to do with that idiotic drug story you've been working on," Harry said, standing behind me. "Told you it was going to be nothing but trouble. For all we know, the Colombia drug cartel broke in here last night."

"Oh, for godsake, Harry." I sighed deeply, feeling much too tired to have this argument yet again. I'd been through too much in the last twelve hours. "First of all, if those guys had been the Colombia drug cartel, they never would've been scared off by your ten-dollar-an-hour rent-a-cop and his toy gun. They'd have shot him dead and kept right on looking for whatever they were looking for. And second, I've shelved that damned drug story. I'm onto something else that's more timely. So get off my case, will you?"

"So you finally came to your senses. You're dropping that suicidal drug nonsense."

"I didn't say that. I said I'd shelved the story. For now." No way was I going to admit I was going to have to find someone younger to help me research the local club scene.

"So what else are you up to? What did you do to make somebody mad enough to break in here and rummage through your file cabinet?"

"If I knew that, I could tell fortunes on the pier and I wouldn't have to work here for a living. Hell, you write stories that expose people's foibles, they're going to get pissed off every so often. Goes with the territory, Harry. Or have you been selling ads instead of practicing journalism for so long you forgot all about that?"

I shooed Harry out of my office and tried to slam the door in a fit of pique but, as usual, it stuck against its bent frame, still open a couple of inches. Somehow that defect always ruins the impact.

I slumped down in my chair, plopped my elbows on my desk and held my aching head in my hands, refusing to let myself cry again. What the hell was going on? And why couldn't I see it?

"What's the matter, dear?"

I looked up a few minutes later to see Lucy pushing my

door open, a steaming cup of coffee in her hand. She set it on my desk and slid it across to me. She looked so kind and sympathetic that I told her precisely what was wrong.

"Why that's awful!" she said when I'd finished. "Your whole house is in a shambles?"

"There has to be a connection, Lucy," I said. "I hate to admit it, but Harry's right. I'll have to tell him, but I'm not in the mood for anymore yelling right now. Whatever's going on here, it's about me, about something I've written, probably, or questions I've been asking. But I can't figure out what it is or what to do about it."

"Don't worry, I'll tell Harry after he cools down a bit," she said in her best mothering voice. "So, if you did know what this was about, Quinn, what would you do?"

"I—I don't know. I guess I'd call the police and tell them who to arrest for wrecking my house."

"Good. That's a first positive step." She nodded approvingly. "So as soon as you figure out who did this, you'll have him arrested. And what else?"

"I don't know what else."

"Would you write a retraction of a story you've already printed, or change whatever new thing you're working on?"

"Hell no! I'm not printing any retraction unless what I wrote was definitely wrong, and nobody's going to intimidate me off a story. I'm a journalist."

Lucy smiled for the first time since I'd arrived that morning. "Then it seems there's only one thing to do right now."

"Such as?"

"Go back to work. If you ever figure out who the villain is, Quinn, fine, call the police. But if you don't, at least you'll have written some more good stories."

"Why didn't I think of that?"

"You're just tired, dear. It's perfectly understandable. Now drink your coffee before it gets cold."

I did.

By the time I got home late that afternoon, the disaster cleanup people were busily scooping broken dishes and cups, as well as a good part of my wardrobe, into a small dumpster. I spent an hour digging through the rubble to find things I wanted to keep, damaged or not: the sole photo I have of me with my parents; a script my father wrote before he was blacklisted; my parents' wedding album; a few of my favorite books.

Not everything I owned had been ruined, of course, not the way it would have been in a fire or flood. In that way, I was lucky. Some of my clothes had survived intact, as had much of what was stored on the kitchen shelves. Most of the furniture was either undamaged or could be repaired. Maybe things weren't as bad as I'd thought last night. A coat of paint and new carpeting would do wonders for this place. My little guesthouse had been ready for those improvements even before last night's invasion. Now at least a partial renovation could no longer be postponed.

As for my clothes, many of them were either becoming outdated or fit me a bit too snugly, anyway. It wouldn't kill me to buy some new things, especially if the insurance company would foot part of the bill.

By the time I got back to the main house, Teddy had dinner ready to put on the table. "Syl's coming over after dinner, just for dessert. I baked a boysenberry pie," he informed me.

I could almost feel my waistline expanding as I thought about that pie. "You've got to stop baking all these goodies or I'll get so fat I'll need another new wardrobe next month," I told him.

"Nonsense. I used my low-sugar recipe, and boysenberries are full of Vitamin C."

Right, like my real problem was a vitamin deficiency, not battling middle-age spread. At least the main meal Teddy'd prepared was light—a bowl of fragrant mushroom soup, some crusty sourdough bread, and a crisp green salad.

As we ate, I told him about the research I'd been doing into Shane King's and Tiffany Novotny's deaths.

"So you think the break-in had something to do with ruffling the wrong people's feathers on that story?" Teddy dunked a corner of his bread in his soup.

"If not that, I can't imagine what else. Pierce Ireland went to his lawyer when he wanted to get back at me, so why would he resort to vandalism after he'd already filed a lawsuit?"

"Good point, unless he's had to call off the lawsuit. Could be his lawyer told him he didn't have a case, once he saw that spreadsheet Harry faxed over. If Ireland lost his job and then his lawyer dumped his case on top of it, he might well be angry enough to do something like this."

"But apparently there were two guys who broke into the *Star*'s office. The security guard saw both of them hightailing it out of there when they saw the flashing lights on his cruiser. If this is Ireland's doing, who's the buddy he had with him?"

Teddy didn't have any ideas about that. "Say, here's another thought—what about that investment-dollars-for-visas scheme you've been researching?" he asked. "Could there be a connection to that?"

I considered Teddy's suggestion for a moment. "Seems to me Henry Fong's dancing on some pretty dicey legal ground," I said, "but I have to do a lot of research on immigration law before I'll know for sure. And, so far, the INS doesn't seem inclined to do anything about Fong's little foreign exchange program, assuming they're aware of it."

Exactly how the Chinese-American producer's scam worked wasn't clear to me yet. All I knew was that he seemed to have found a way to entice rich Hong Kong businessmen who wanted to emigrate to the U.S. to invest big bucks in his movies. In return, Fong signed documents saying he'd hired these very same investors as essential workers on his productions. Their skills supposedly were both invaluable to his movies and impossible to find in an American worker.

So, with an investment of half a million or more in one of Fong's pictures, anybody who wanted to leave Hong Kong and become a legal U.S. resident could do it. The work visas they needed to enter the country and stay here were fast-tracked because of their unique abilities. Yet, as far as I could tell, not one of these invaluable workers ever came near either Fong or one of his movie sets after they arrived in America.

"I don't think I'm far enough along on that story to have stepped on any important toes," I told Teddy, "at least not hard enough to be personally attacked." I reached for a second piece of bread. "I'm just getting started."

"Come to think of it, tearing apart your home doesn't really sound like the way a man like Henry Fong would choose to intimidate you," Teddy said. "He'd more likely try to bribe you. And if that didn't get you to abandon your story, he'd probably hire a hit man."

"Great! Something else to look forward to." I shook my head no as Teddy offered me another helping of soup. "Saving room for a taste of your pie. So where does all this leave me? Back with Shane and Tiffany, right?"

"Or with somebody else whose nose is out of joint because of something you wrote." Teddy used his napkin to wipe up a drop of soup that had spilled on the dining room table when he'd ladled his second helping out of the tureen. "But that's a pretty long list, isn't it?"

Lord, I felt popular—half of Hollywood hated me enough to trash my home. And, if it hadn't been for the alarm system at work, my office there would have been ruined, too. "Say it does have to do with Shane and Tiffany," I said. "What I don't understand is why anybody would want the two of them dead in the first place. If Shane was a screw-up, all anybody had to do was fire him, or stop seeing him socially, or not return his phone calls, whatever. They certainly didn't have to kill him to get rid of him. And so what if Tiffany was a self-obsessed little twit? All anybody had to do was ignore her, not kill her."

"So if this vandalism has something to do with those dead kids, you don't really know why?"

"I thought for a while there might some connection with that girl Rhett was partying with on the night she was murdered," I said. "Peter told me Rhett was never the same again after it happened, that Lauren Hartley's death marked his descent into heavy drug use. But what could that night possibly have to do with Tiffany? She was only a child, living on a farm near Salinas back then. Even Shane was linked to the rape and murder only by the fact his older brother was there."

"How much younger was Shane than Rhett?" Teddy asked. "I'm thinking Shane might have been at the beach that night, too."

I did the math in my head. "They were four years apart, so Shane would still have been in junior high. I suppose it's possible he was partying with the older kids, but I really doubt it. What high school senior would want somebody's kid brother hanging around, especially if they were all drinking and getting high?"

"They wouldn't, but maybe Shane sneaked into that party, invited or not."

I didn't buy that, either. Veronica King hadn't been a bad mother, as far as I know, just an impossible wife, if you could believe Peter's account of their marriage. I doubted she'd let her thirteen-year-old son stay out all night at a beach party. She was probably worried enough about letting her seventeen-year-old do it.

Still, everything I could think of seemed to point to Palisades High School. Maybe that counselor Lucy'd talked to there could tell me more about these kids. She'd certainly seemed forthcoming when Lucy spoke to her.

As Sylvia let herself in the front door, dressed in a flowing brilliant purple gown, a bottle of port wine in her hand, I made a mental note to talk to Hannah Ruiz in the morning. For now, I would force myself to stop thinking about anything but my slice of boysenberry pie.

"I remember both the King boys quite well," Hannah Ruiz told me the next morning. She'd agreed to see me during the third period of the school day, which was generally her lunch break. Now we were sitting in her office, a square little room with a full wall of file cabinets. Its one attractive feature was a view of the hillside and a small peek of the ocean from the sole window. "Rhett and Shane were only average students," she added, "but I still thought they'd do well in life, given their connections."

"But now they're both dead," I said.

"Sometimes you just can't predict how things will turn

out," she said with a small shake of her head. "Doesn't stop us from trying, though, does it?"

The Palisades High School counselor was a dark-haired, tiny woman, no taller than five-one or -two, and she probably didn't weigh a hundred pounds stepping out of the shower. I felt like a pale giant next to her. I pegged her at about my own age. She'd started her counseling career at Pali right after college graduation and, twenty years later, she was still here. She'd pulled the school files on both Shane and Rhett King and seemed anxious to share whatever information she had on the two dead brothers.

"Over the years you've been at Pali, Ms. Ruiz, you certainly must have seen plenty of kids here who messed around with drugs," I said. "What about Rhett and Shane?"

"Rhett used alcohol, I'm positive about that, and probably marijuana as well. Nothing harder until his senior year. Then he seemed to go off the deep end." She referred to some papers in her file. "Here it is. Senior year he was absent twenty-seven times, and there are eight reports here of him falling asleep in class. Almost didn't graduate."

My guess was the school would have done almost anything to graduate a student like Rhett King, even if he never came to class. He was one of the affluent, well-connected locals whose families could make big trouble for the high school's staff if he'd been held back. "And what about Shane?" I asked.

She opened the other file and leafed through it. "Shane was a bit of a behavior problem, but not because of drugs, at least not as far as I could tell. My take on it was that the boy was severely depressed after his brother died. His way of coping was to take out his rage on other kids, usually ones smaller than he was. He was way too confrontational with everybody, always right in your face. Got into lots of fights, most of which he provoked. Frequently belligerent with his teachers, too. I'm afraid Shane King had one of the worst detention records of anyone in his class."

"But no drugs."

Ruiz shook her head. "I honestly don't think so. I didn't see any of the usual signs in him." A pretty woman, she had shiny dark hair that fell in loose curls to her shoulders and a face that seemed almost overwhelmed by her big brown eyes.

"There are a few other students I'd like to ask you about, too," I said. "Is that okay?"

She glanced at the clock on the wall. "As long as we don't get into areas that are confidential. With Rhett and Shane, I'm not worried—they're both dead—but I have to be more careful with the others."

"Lauren Hartley," I said, figuring we might as well start with another student whose secrets were now dead and buried.

"The girl who was murdered," Ruiz said, her big eyes narrowing. "Why do you want to know about her?"

"I'm asking as a reporter, but I'm also a friend of Peter King, Rhett and Shane's father. Peter told me that Rhett got into drugs very heavily right after Lauren Hartley's death. It obviously affected him deeply. So maybe there's a connection between her murder and the King boys' deaths." It wasn't much of an explanation, but Ruiz seemed to accept it.

"As I remember, Lauren was quite a pretty girl, blond and slim, but also very quiet and shy. Can't say I knew her very well. Basically, like most of our students here at Pali, she never got into trouble, so she didn't stand out in the crowd. The ones I remember most vividly all stood out, a few because they were exceptionally good students or because they had famous parents, but far more because I had to counsel them about their problem behavior."

"Do you recall if Lauren used drugs or drank or maybe had a reputation for being promiscuous?"

Ruiz went to her wall of file cabinets, opened a low drawer, and pulled out another student file. "Some of what you're asking I wouldn't be in a position to know, not if it didn't impact on Lauren's hours at school." She glanced through the paperwork. "She doesn't seem like the type for any of that acting-out behavior. Member of the choir, worked on the school plays, though only as a costume maker or lighting technician. Maybe she was too shy to be on stage herself. Belonged to the French Club, volunteered at an old age home. Good student—a B-plus average. There's no indication she ever sought counseling, either for a personal problem or for help with her college applications. Sorry I can't remember more about her."

"That's okay. I'd also like to know anything you can remember about the boy who murdered her, Luis Alvarez."

For the first time, Ruiz seemed to bristle. "I don't believe Luis *is* a murderer," she said. "I don't care what the court said. If Luis killed Lauren, it must have been some kind of freak accident."

"But she was sexually assaulted and strangled, Ms. Ruiz. It's pretty hard to make that into an accidental death."

Ruiz chewed her lower lip. "I can't explain that. If they were having consensual sex, maybe something went wrong. Or if she really was raped, there supposedly were other boys with Luis that night. Maybe they're the ones who raped and killed her. I don't know, except I just can't see Luis as a rapist or murderer. He was such a nice, gentle boy. A violent act like that just wasn't in his character."

"But if Luis was wrongfully accused, why did he confess?

Why didn't he tell the police what really happened?"

She shook her head. "I don't know. Bad legal advice, maybe, or fear of retaliation." She sighed deeply. "Or maybe I'm indulging in wishful thinking. Luis *did* confess, didn't he? Maybe he actually did this horrible thing after all. I suppose it's possible he got high on some drug and turned into a different person, but it's still almost impossible for me to believe he's guilty.

"He was a model student here, exactly what we all were hoping for when we started busing in kids from the poorer parts of L.A." She removed another file from her cabinets. "Here it is." She opened it. "Luis had a three-point-eight grade point average, an A-minus. He particularly excelled in writing and photography, planned on going to college, maybe becoming a novelist or a photojournalist. He had his whole future mapped out.

"There's not one report of any misbehavior in his file. Sure, he came from a poor neighborhood and his mother was stuck raising him and two younger children by herself, with no father in the home, but that's why Luis was trying so hard to make something of his life. He wanted out of the ghetto and he wanted to take his mom and his sisters with him. It just doesn't make sense that he'd risk his big dream, not to mention all his hard work, by raping and killing a rich blond classmate."

I rattled off the names of the other students who'd been identified by the *Times* as being part of the beach party—Troy Kellerman, Julia Jackson, Joseph Taliaferro, Stevenson Brooks.

"The ones whose addresses your secretary wanted," Ruiz said, wrinkling her nose. "The school elite."

"Elite?"

"Extremely wealthy kids who lived up in the hills, in

houses with panoramic views and swimming pools, pampered by their folks, phoning it in in their classes, plenty of attitude."

"As opposed to Luis Alvarez." I wondered whether the fact Ruiz and Luis were of the same ethnic heritage had colored the counselor's judgment.

"Look, Luis was gentle and kind. I never heard him make fun of another student, not once. Those others, though, they relished the putdown, loved making kids who had less than they did squirm. A real nasty bunch of mouths on that crew."

"All of them?"

Ruiz nodded. "Pretty much, except maybe Julia and Lauren—they seemed a lot more decent than the boys. High school can be torture for kids who are different, Ms. Quinn. And the worst torturers are often youngsters like the ones you just named, the students who've had everything handed to them, who feel superior to others who haven't had it so easy. Bullies like them think they're entitled to look down on people like Luis Alvarez. You ask me, it ought to be precisely the other way around."

I couldn't argue that point. I've been put down too often in my own life not to know how it feels. "Are you still in touch with Luis, Ms. Ruiz?" I asked.

Her face softened and her big eyes grew moist. "He used to write me every couple of weeks from Soledad Prison, and I'd write back to him, let him know what was going on at school, that sort of thing. But then he stopped. I guess our correspondence probably became painful in a way. It must have reminded him of everything he lost when he was sent away to prison."

We talked for a few minutes about the other students I'd mentioned and I took a few notes, then Hannah Ruiz glanced at the clock and told me we were out of time.

I got to my feet. "Thanks so much for taking the time to answer my questions," I said, shaking her delicate hand. "I really appreciate it."

"I don't really know if I was any help but, if you see Shane's dad, will you tell him how sorry I am for his loss? It has to be sheer agony, losing both his sons that way."

"He's definitely having some trouble with that," I admitted. "I'll be sure to tell him you sent your sympathy."

As I opened the office door, an ear-splitting bell announced the end of third period and a mass of students spilled out of the classrooms and into the hallway.

I caught up with Julia Jackson just as she was leaving her apartment at the edge of the campus of California State University Northridge, in the San Fernando Valley. CSUN had been at the epicenter of the big Northridge earthquake, which severely damaged or destroyed many of the school's buildings. Years later, many classes still were being held in the low brown prefab buildings brought in as temporary classrooms after the quake. Some of the permanent buildings still hadn't been sufficiently retrofitted to make them safe enough to use.

I quickly explained who I was and that I wanted to ask Julia a few questions.

"Sorry, I really can't talk to you now," she said as she stepped into the hallway and locked her apartment door. "I've got class in twenty minutes and I have to walk halfway across campus." Hannah Ruiz had told me Julia'd spent several years taking a course or two a semester, partying and playing at being a student, before finally settling down and becoming serious about college. Now, several years older than most of her fellow students, she was a senior majoring in political science at CSUN.

"I'll walk to class with you," I offered. "We can talk on the way."

Julia shrugged her shoulders as if to say it was a free world, she couldn't stop me from walking. "I walk pretty fast," she warned. She was a tall brunette, reed slim, with a narrow face and intelligent green eyes.

"Don't worry. I've got long legs," I said. "I'll try to keep up with you."

We chatted about the world of politics and government for a few minutes as we headed out of her apartment building into the hot, smoggy air. Like many political science majors, Julia confided that her goal was to work in Washington, D.C., maybe even run for political office herself someday.

"So what exactly did you want to see me about?" she asked as we headed onto the campus, an eclectic collection of buildings even before the quake. Now several of them were framed by scaffolding. The walking paths between buildings were crowded with students, all scurrying to class.

"I'm working on a story for the *Star* and it requires some research about Shane King," I told her. "I thought you might be able to help me."

"Rhett's kid brother." Julia sighed deeply and her stride slowed a bit, as though she was suddenly carrying an extra twenty pounds on her shoulders. "I saw in the *Times* that Shane died," she said, giving me a suspicious look. "Isn't it a little late for you to be doing research on him?"

I could see I wasn't going to be able to gloss over my real motivations, not with Julia Jackson. She was a poli sci student and, if her professors had taught her anything at all, it had to be how a spin could be put on a story. "I honestly don't know yet whether there's a story here, but there's a question about just how Shane died," I told her, "about whether it was an accidental overdose, suicide, or possibly even murder. Shane's dad is a friend of mine and he asked me to dig into it. I'm starting with people who knew his brother and why he OD'd."

Julia suddenly stopped short. A short, chubby youth carrying a mammoth backpack slammed into her, almost knocking her down. "Hey, watch where you're walking!" she yelled at him.

"Watch where you're standing!" he retorted. "You stopped dead right in front of me!"

As I took Julia's elbow and steered her off the path onto the grass, I could feel her shaking. "Let's stand over here, out of traffic, for a bit." I glanced at my watch. "You've still got fifteen minutes before your class starts." When I glanced up again, I noticed Julia's eyes were filled with tears. "Hey, did that guy hurt you?" I asked.

"No, it's not him. It's just that—I—I—I try not to think about Rhett or—or about what happened to Lauren Hartley. You'd think, after all this time and all the therapy I've had, I'd be over it by now. And now you say Shane . . ."

"It's hard to get over a good friend's death."

"It's a lot more than that," Julia said, blinking hard. "Rhett King was my boyfriend, up until Lauren got killed, anyway. He was the first guy I—the first man I ever really loved. Then Lauren got killed and he changed, almost overnight, into somebody I didn't even know."

"That's when Rhett began using hard drugs, isn't it?"

Julia nodded, wiping her cheeks. "We broke up a few weeks after Lauren died. He wouldn't even see me anymore. I felt abandoned, and I—I felt really responsible for—"

"For what?"

"For Lauren's being killed."

"Why, Julia? How could her death be your fault?"

"Because she would never have been at that stupid party if it hadn't been for me. Lauren was my best friend. She was a really smart, funny girl, but she was very shy, particularly around guys. I don't think she ever had a real date in her whole life. I thought maybe I could help her meet somebody, that if Rhett and I brought her along to that party, she might find a guy of her own."

"But things didn't turn out that way."

"Hell, no. Turned out Lauren and I were the only two girls there, and it wasn't even a big group, not at all what I expected. It was all about who could drink the most vodka and smoke the most weed. Lauren was, I don't know, maybe overwhelmed is the word. She kept giving me this look all night, like what the hell did you get me into?"

"Did Lauren drink and smoke with the others?"

"A little maybe, not much. She was trying not to make a scene about what was going on, but I could tell she wanted us to take her home. If only . . ."

"Did you see Luis Alvarez and his friends that night?"

"Just Luis, nobody else. He was walking on the beach and stopped to say hi to us. He was in my geometry class at Pali, and he seemed nice enough. Rhett and Lauren and I were polite to him, but Troy and Joe and Steve, they started ragging on him, so he left."

"The newspaper stories said there was a whole group of people with Luis."

"Not that I saw. That happened later. Truth is, Rhett and I had way too much to drink and we started feeling it. We took our beach blanket down the sand a ways, sort of cuddled up on it, and fell asleep." She grimaced. "Passed out's probably more like it, to tell the truth. When we woke up and came back to the party, the boys were all zonked to the gills and Lauren wasn't with them. I asked where she was, and the others said she'd gone for a walk, that they hadn't seen her for a while."

"What about the gang of Latinos?"

Julia nodded. "They said Luis came back with some of his homies, that the Chicanos were acting like they wanted to start a fight."

"Did they?"

"Apparently not. Just talked a bunch of trash, ripped off Steve's stash of weed, and split."

"Yet they claimed Lauren went off on her own when your group had already had trouble. Why would she do that?"

"Joe said she got mad at him and Troy and Steve, accused them of being a bunch of racist snobs because they dissed the Chicanos. Troy said he figured maybe Lauren went off to find Luis, to apologize to him and his friends."

"Does that sound logical to you, like something Lauren would do?"

Julia stared at the ground. "She certainly would have been upset if anybody was using racial slurs—Lauren didn't have a bigoted bone in her body, she hated bigots. But I can't really see her going off by herself like that, not on the beach in the dark. Unless she went looking for me to take her home."

"What happened next?"

"Nothing, at first. When Lauren still didn't come back maybe half an hour later, I started getting really scared. I told the guys we couldn't wait anymore, we had to go find her."

"And you found her dead."

"Not me, thank God. Rhett and Troy did. But they

wouldn't call the police, not until they could get rid of our drugs and booze and we had enough time to sober up. Said it wasn't going to make any difference to Lauren how fast the police got there, and there was no reason they should get busted over this, it wasn't their fault she was dead."

"So how long was it before they called the police?"

Julia shook her head. "I don't know. Maybe another half hour, maybe an hour. I was still pretty groggy. When they told me what happened to Lauren, I got sick to my stomach, puked all over our beach blanket. We threw it in a trash can before the cops got there."

"So, do you think the Latinos' attack on Lauren was retaliation for the way your group had treated Luis and his friends earlier?"

Julia glanced at her watch. "Look, I honestly don't know, okay? I really do have to get to class; I can't be late." She darted back onto the path and resumed walking.

I was barely able to keep up as she increased her stride. The smoggy air made me feel short of breath, but Julia seemed to be used to it. Or maybe the difference was just that she was a good fifteen years younger than I was. "Still see any of those kids you went to Pali with?" I asked.

"Not really," Julia said, "except for Ginger Gleason. Ginger Fariday's her name now—she's married and has this perfectly adorable baby girl. Ginger used to be pretty wild in high school, but she's changed a lot since then. Lives just a couple of blocks away from me. We ran into each other at an AA meeting a couple of years ago and now we're pretty close friends."

"But you don't see Troy or Steve or Joe anymore?"

"Hell, no, not if I can avoid it. Bunch of sexist, racist assholes, you ask me. Boy, Ginger sure could tell you a thing or two about those creeps."

"Like what?" I asked as we arrived in front of one of the low brown temporary buildings.

Julia turned to me, her cheeks beginning to color. "Hey, forget I even mentioned it. Anything I know is all second-hand gossip anyway. I'm afraid I already blabbed way too much." She shifted her stack of books to her other arm. "Hey, Ms. Collins, if you do write something about Shane, I'd sure appreciate it if you didn't put in anything about how drunk I used to get. Can we keep that much off the record? I've worked really hard to change my life—I'm sober for more than three years now. And none of that stuff has anything to do with Shane King, anyhow."

She looked like she was about to break into tears again. "I'll do my best to keep your name out of it, Julia," I promised. "And, hey, thanks for talking to me. I wish you luck getting the kind of job you want when you graduate."

"Thanks." She took a deep breath, squared her slender shoulders, and slipped through the door into her classroom.

I walked back to my car at a much slower pace and, at the gas station on the corner, I spotted a pay phone that actually still had a phone directory attached to it. Leafing through the white pages, I found a listing for Fariday, Glenn and Ginger, with an address near the campus. I took a notepad and pencil from my purse and copied down the information.

Julia Jackson's comment had piqued my interest. I might be far afield from finding out anything about how either Shane or Tiffany died, but sometimes, I've learned, you just have to go with what your gut tells you. If nothing else, I was curious about what Ginger Fariday could tell me about Troy Kellerman, Stevenson Brooks, and Joseph Taliaferro.

I found the young mother in the backyard of her small

pinkish beige stucco tract house, a common type of structure in the San Fernando Valley. She was sitting on the grass next to a tiny inflatable plastic swimming pool, watching her toddler play in the water.

"Can I help you?" she asked as I rounded the corner of her house. She was a petite young woman, with bright red hair and blue eyes. I wondered whether she'd been named Ginger because of her hair color or if she'd dyed her hair that particular shade because it suited her name. Her baby's hair was medium brown without a touch of the mother's russet tones.

"Nobody answered the door," I replied, "but I thought I heard some noise from back here. Are you Ginger Fariday?"

"You found me, but whatever you're selling, you're wasting your time, lady. I don't care if it's cosmetics or herbal supplements or religion, I'm not buying any."

The baby slapped her tiny hands against the surface of the little pool, giggling as the water splashed upward. The bridge of the child's nose was beginning to turn a bit pink. I hoped Ginger knew enough to coat her baby daughter with sun block.

"Julia was absolutely right," I said, flashing Ginger a smile. "Your baby really is adorable. What's her name?"

"Emma." Ginger eyed me suspiciously. "You talking about Julia Jackson?"

"Right. I just spoke to her, over at CSUN." I squatted down on the grass next to the plastic pool and introduced myself. "I'm working on a story for the *Star*, Ginger, and the names of some guys you and Julia used to know at Pali High have come up in my research. She seemed to think you could tell me plenty about them."

"Yeah?" She shot me that suspicious look again. "Who?"

"Rhett King, Joe Taliaferro, Troy Kellerman, and Steve Brooks."

"What about them?"

"Julia indicated that some of them were pretty bad guys, but she says you know more about that than she does."

"Maybe. I don't know all that much about Rhett. He seemed okay, until he turned into a junkie. Julia probably told you she used to date him. Rhett's dead now, he OD'd, but I'm sure you already know that. The rest of that crew, I wouldn't give two cents to save any of their necks."

"Julia has pretty much the same attitude. What exactly was their problem?"

"How come she didn't tell you?"

"Said she had only second-hand information, that whatever she knew she'd learned from you."

"Why do you want to know?"

I gave her the same explanation I'd given Julia.

Ginger handed a plastic duck to Emma, who dunked it in the water over and over again, laughing with glee each time it bobbed to the surface again.

"Look," Ginger said, avoiding eye contact. "This is ancient history, a lot of stuff I've tried really hard to forget. I was incredibly dumb to think I could make those boys like me, okay? But I'm married now, I've got a kid, and I'm going to make sure she grows up a whole lot smarter than me." She shuddered. "I don't even like to think about high school anymore. It's like a bad dream."

"It couldn't have been all bad, could it? What makes it so hard for you to remember the good parts?"

"The goddamned Pali Playboys and that goddamned scorecard of theirs, that's what."

"Pali Playboys? Who're they?"

Ginger thought for a moment while she chewed on a

thumbnail. "Shit," she mumbled under her breath. "You won't put my name in your article, right?"

"Not if you ask me not to."

"Because, if you're going to use my name, I won't tell you a thing. I've got a husband now, I've got almost all different friends. I don't want them reading all my secrets in your newspaper."

"I won't use your name, Ginger. I promise you that. And maybe what you have to say isn't even important to my investigation. But I have a hunch it will be."

She stared at me as if trying to tell whether I could really be trusted. Her chin began to quiver a bit, but she bit down hard on her lower lip until she got herself back under control. "Troy was the first one I was with," she said in a low, shaky voice. "I guess he got the full hundred points."

"A hundred points? For what?"

"For fuck—" She glanced at her daughter splashing in the pool and cleaned up her language. "For—for having sex with a virgin. I was stupid enough to believe Troy was in love with me, but as soon as we had sex, he dumped me and started chasing Amy Lawson."

"What do you mean about Troy's getting points? What kind of points?"

Ginger sighed and stared at the grass. "It's all so humiliating. You're absolutely certain you won't use my name?"

"I keep my promises."

"God, I sure hope so. See, it turns out they had this secret club, called themselves the Palisades Playboys. I didn't find out about their dirty little game until way later, of course, not until after I'd already slept with three of the boys in the club, anyway. They were a bunch of rich, spoiled brats who thought it was great fun to trick girls into going to bed with them. Then they compared their—their exploits at their sleazy little meetings. They even set up a point system so they could compete with each other.

"I heard bedding a virgin earned the highest score—the full hundred points. Then, if the girl wasn't a virgin, they earned different points depending on the kind of girl they got—higher points for pretty girls, lower for ugly ones or fat ones or minorities. The point total they earned depended on what kind of sex it was, too, you know, the—the position."

My jaw was hanging open. "And not one of these girls figured out what was going on?" I was stunned.

"I didn't, anyway. And I can't believe any of them would have gone along with it, not if they knew they were being used like that, especially if they'd known other guys would be watching them have sex."

"Watching?" It had been a long time since I'd been a teenager. Had sex really become so meaningless that teens nowadays invited their friends to watch them making love?

"Right, watching, like a peeping Tom. The Pali Playboys would bring a girl to their bedroom at home, while their parents were out. One or two other members of the club would hide somewhere they could see what was happening—in the closet, maybe, or outside an open window, like that. That was the way they proved to the other guys that they'd really done it. They had to have somebody else in the club vouch for them."

"How big was this club?" I asked.

"At least five guys I know about. Troy, Joe and Steve, and two others."

"Was Rhett King a member?"

"I don't think so. He acted like he didn't approve, but he knew about it. Used to hang out with those guys sometimes. They all lived in the same neighborhood in the Palisades, knew each other since junior high, their parents were friends, that sort of thing."

"And did this go on the whole time they were in high school?"

Ginger shook her head, her hair blazing in the afternoon sun. "I think it fell apart after that girl Lauren was killed."

"Why?"

She raised a shoulder and let it drop again. "I don't know, really. Maybe sex didn't seem like such innocent fun after she got raped and murdered." Emma tossed the duck into the air and it landed on the grass outside the pool. Ginger picked it up and placed it back in the water. "Here you go, sweet cheeks," she said.

"Did you know Lauren Hartley?" I asked.

"Just to say hello to. I remember the kids used to call her the nun."

"Why's that?"

"Because she was so straight, I guess, and she always dressed so conservatively. Or maybe she wanted to be a real nun someday, I don't know."

"So you don't think she was the type to be having sex with the Pali Playboys."

"God, no. In fact, when I heard how she was killed, I couldn't figure out what she was doing on the beach with those guys."

"Julia told me she and Rhett brought Lauren along with them that night, that they'd expected it to be a big beach party where Lauren might meet somebody."

"Yeah, Julia told me the same thing, that one time we talked about it. I'm afraid poor Julia still feels guilty, like it's her fault Lauren got killed, when all she really did is try to find her a boyfriend."

I nodded. "I guess we all have things in our pasts we regret, things we need to learn to forgive ourselves for."

Ginger gave her daughter a wistful look. "Time to get out of the water, pumpkin," she said, pushing herself into a standing position. "It's nap time, and we can't let you get sunburned, can we?" She spread a large blue towel on the grass and lifted Emma onto it, then wrapped it around the squirming baby and dried her off.

"Thanks for your time," I said to Ginger, recognizing that I was being dismissed.

"Hope it helps."

"I don't know how yet, but I'm sure it will. And don't worry, I'm not going to use your name."

"Thanks." She stood up and lifted Emma onto her hip. "You know," she said, turning to face me, "it's a damn good thing they caught that Chicano kid and he confessed that he killed Lauren."

"I guess it—"

"Otherwise, you'd really have to wonder, wouldn't you?"

"About what?"

"About what kind of score the Palisades Playboys would rack up for gang banging a virgin."

I watched as she carried Emma through the backdoor of her little house and pulled the door closed behind her. After she'd gone, I stood in the tiny backyard for a moment longer, thinking about everything Ginger Fariday had just told me.

Despite the Valley's smoggy afternoon heat, I suddenly felt chilled to the bone.

9

By the time I got back to the office, the rest of the *Hollywood Star*'s staff was ready to leave for the day, but I didn't mind. I work more efficiently when I have the place to myself anyway.

I phoned in a delivery order to my favorite Chinese restaurant, then settled in at my desk for a late night. After three hours and far more cashew chicken than I had any business eating, I'd managed to produce three articles for this week's *Star*, plus a thick batch of fillers. Except for information I'd gleaned from a couple of quick telephone interviews, I'd used far more press release hype than I like to, but at least the *Star* wouldn't have to run four pages short this week because of my extracurricular activities.

After I'd finished my work and left a detailed note for our photographer, telling her what shots we'd need to go with my articles, I took out my file on Shane King and reread the *Times* stories about Lauren Hartley's murder. It was in the fourth story in the series that I finally found what I was looking for, a mention of Luis Alvarez's attorney. He'd been represented by a public defender named Madeleine Raymond. It was too late to contact Raymond now, but at least I could use my computer to access the California Bar Association's list of attorneys.

It didn't take me long to find her. No longer with the public defender's office, Madeleine Raymond was now a partner at Borland, O'Neil & Krantz, a law firm in Century City. She'd obviously moved up in the world. Way up.

* * * * *

When I phoned Madeleine Raymond's office the next morning, her secretary told me she would be in court in Santa Monica all day. I worked in the office until eleven, then drove the short distance to the Santa Monica courthouse and sat in the back of the courtroom.

Raymond was a large-boned, muscular woman in her mid- to late-thirties, slightly buck-toothed, with tightly permed brown hair and a perpetually sour expression on her face. She reminded me of my fourth grade teacher, Miss Durbin, an unsmiling disciplinarian who was universally disliked by her students. But I tried not to prejudge the lawyer simply because of her resemblance to my childhood nemesis.

This morning, Raymond was defending a stockbroker being sued for defrauding a group of elderly investors, a middle-aged man wearing a thousand-dollar suit. He was no Michael Milken, apparently, but as a client he had to be a giant leap upward from the destitute bunch Raymond had represented as a public defender. Her own dove gray business suit looked like it had cost nearly as much as her client's garb, and it wasn't hard to see her financial status had improved greatly over the past decade.

I found what I observed of the trial to be incredibly tedious. As Raymond and the plaintiffs' attorney questioned an expert witness about short sales, futures, and junk bonds—all financial gibberish to me—I waited impatiently for the judge to announce the lunch break and tried my best not to doze off.

When the recess finally arrived, I waylaid the defense attorney before she could escape from the courtroom.

"I need to ask you a few questions about a former client of yours," I told her after introducing myself briefly, "a young man named Luis Alvarez."

"Who?" Raymond asked, visibly annoyed at being accosted by one of those pesky reporters.

"Luis Alvarez, the teenager who was convicted of raping and murdering a girl named Lauren Hartley at the beach about ten years ago. They were both students at Palisades High School."

She frowned. "Ten years ago, I was working in the public defender's office," she said.

"Yes, I know that. You were Luis Alvarez's defense attorney."

She sighed deeply. "Do you have any idea how many cases I handled when I was a PD?"

"I'm sure quite a few."

"Literally thousands. Some days I had thirty open cases on my desk, *thirty!* Public defenders work their asses off and they get paid crap. It's like working on some factory assembly line. No way could I possibly remember all the people I represented."

"I take it that means you don't remember Luis Alvarez."

She shook her head. Her Brillo-pad hair didn't even quiver. "Sorry, I can't help you." She started to walk away.

"Luis plea bargained to second degree murder," I said, staying by her side as she strode out of the courtroom and down the hallway of the courthouse. "He got twenty-five to life, but some people don't think he's guilty."

"Sure. His mother, maybe? Or his girlfriend? Look, there's always somebody who believes the accused is innocent, that he couldn't possibly have done such an evil thing. But if we plea bargained this guy down to a lesser charge, I can pretty well guarantee you he did the deed."

Or, I was beginning to think, maybe the kid's freebie attorney was just too damned busy to give him a proper defense. I curbed my tongue, however, figuring there was no percentage in ticking off this woman any more than I already had. "You must have files on all your old cases," I suggested.

"Back at the PD's office. I'd need a moving van and an extra storage room to take them with me."

The woman obviously was still angry about the workload she'd carried as a public defender. Or maybe she was the kind of person who's perpetually angry about everything.

"You still have access to those files, though, right?" I asked.

She shot me a look of utter disgust. "Look, I'm in the middle of an important case here, and I've got a cross-examination to prepare," she said. "I simply don't have time to deal with this."

"Luis Alvarez, on the other hand, has nothing but time, Ms. Raymond." She was starting to tick me off, too. "He's already been in prison for nearly a decade, and he's got another fifteen years to go. In the meantime, there've been two more murders, and there's some pretty credible evidence they were committed by the same people who killed Lauren Hartley. One of those people was definitely *not* Luis." What the hell, I figured, overstating my evidence was no big sin. A little exaggeration in the service of justice could be excused, couldn't it? "If that young man really is innocent," I told her, "I'm sure you wouldn't want it on your conscience that you did nothing to help clear him."

"This is a story you're investigating for your newspaper?"

I nodded.

"Why? What's it got to do with show business?"

"Both the people who were murdered a short while ago worked in the industry. Also, I promised the father of one of the victims I'd look into it."

"Hmmm. So, if it turns out you're right, and somebody else murdered that girl, what would you say about me in your paper?"

Finally, I could see how to play Madeleine Raymond. "That would depend entirely on how much help I get from you," I told her. "You could come off looking pretty good and, as I'm sure you know, the *Star*'s readership includes most of Hollywood's movers and shakers. My article could bring you and your firm some high-roller clients."

She thought it over.

"On the other hand," I continued, "if you refuse to help me find out the truth, whatever I write might not be at all helpful to your law career."

"Sounds a bit like blackmail to me."

I put on my innocent face. "Oh, not at all, Ms. Raymond. Journalism ethics requires me to write the truth, that's all."

"So what, exactly, do you want from me?"

"I want to know how and why Alvarez ended up with that plea bargain, and what kind of evidence there was that he committed the crime in the first place. Also, why he refused to name any of the friends who were alleged to be with him at the beach on the night of the murder."

"Tell you what I'll do—I'll send my paralegal over to the PD's office to make a copy of the case file. As soon as I have a chance to review it, I'll give you a call."

"That would be very helpful." I took out one of my cards and added my cell phone number to the back of it. "I should caution you, though. I'm on a deadline, so the sooner you can get back to me, the better for both of us. You can reach me any time, day or night."

She took my card. "I'll do the best I can," she said. As

she walked away down the hall, I saw her pull her cell phone out of her briefcase, turn it on, and punch in a number.

It was seven-thirty and I was helping Uncle Teddy clean up the kitchen after dinner when my cell phone rang. It was Madeleine Raymond.

"I—I took a look at the file on the Luis Alvarez case," she said, her voice now sounding far less strident than it had at the courthouse this morning. "It's hard to talk about it over the phone—I'm afraid the case is rather complicated. I know it's late, Ms. Collins, but I have to be in court all day again tomorrow. I wondered if—if you might be able to meet me at my office tonight."

I told her I'd be there in half an hour. Teddy, as usual, was understanding about my sticking him with the cleanup duties.

Borland, O'Neil & Krantz was on the seventeenth floor of one of the Century City office towers. I parked in the underground garage, which I figured would cost me at least ten bucks, and headed for the elevator.

I found attorney Raymond alone in the luxurious suite of offices. She led me into her private office, which faced east and enjoyed a panoramic view of the lights of Los Angeles.

"I expect this is a little different from the digs you had at the public defender's office," I said, admiring the view.

"In more ways than you know. Have a seat," she said, sliding into the chair behind the desk.

I chose one of the two burgundy leather chairs across from her. "So you read the file on Luis Alvarez," I prompted. It was getting late and I was anxious to get back home, take a hot bath and go to bed.

She paused a moment, running her thick fingers through

her tight curls. "Look, Ms. Collins, I honestly want to help you with your story, especially if it might help one of my old clients," she said, "but I'm going to have to ask that you keep my name out of it."

"Why?"

"I think my reasons will become clear enough as we talk. Do I have your word?"

I considered her request. Truth was, I was merely floating a trial balloon here. I had proof of absolutely nothing. And I could think of no good reason I'd ever have to name Madeleine Raymond in any article I might write about Shane and Tiffany. "All right," I agreed. "I won't use your name."

She opened a desk drawer and removed a legal-size file folder. "Oddly enough, I actually do remember this case," she told me. "After I started reviewing it, the details came back to me."

"Was there solid evidence against Luis, Ms. Raymond?"

She looked down at the paperwork. "The evidence consisted almost entirely of the statements of some youths who'd been partying with the victim, Lauren Hartley."

"Let me guess," I said, frowning. "Troy Kellerman, Joseph Taliaferro, and Stevenson Brooks."

"Right. Those three plus a boy named—" She ran her finger down a typed page. "Here it is, the other witness was named Rhett King."

Rhett. I suddenly felt nauseous.

"All four of them told essentially the same story," she said, turning a page in her file. "Said they'd been having a party on the beach when they were approached by a group of Latino youths. One of their classmates, Luis Alvarez, was a member of the group, but they didn't know the others. Claimed the Latinos hassled them for a while, but eventually left. Soon after the Latinos left, the Hartley girl said she was going for a walk on the beach. She didn't come back. When they went to look for her, they found her dead."

"And they told the cops that Luis Alvarez was responsible?"

"They said he'd been coming on to Lauren, but she'd rebuffed him and he was clearly angry about it. They suggested he and his buddies waited until the girl left the protection of her friends, then raped and murdered her."

"And what did Luis say about that?"

"He told a totally different story. Claimed he'd been on the beach alone that night, that he'd spotted his classmates and stopped to say hello. When they didn't ask him to join their party, he left. He said he never even talked to Lauren Hartley, that he knew nothing about her being raped and murdered until the police came to his home the next day to take him downtown for questioning."

"Doesn't sound like there was all that much evidence against the kid," I suggested. "Nobody actually saw him attack the girl, right? So what nailed him, his DNA?"

Raymond leafed through the file and read another of the pages. "There was no sperm found on the body," she told me, "but the girl definitely had been sexually attacked. There were lacerations to both her vagina and her anus, and she had bruises on her face, breasts, and both her wrists and ankles. Looks like she put up a pretty good fight, but she was probably held down while she was raped. The cause of death was asphyxiation."

"No sperm," I said. "So the rapists had to have used condoms."

"Or else the girl was raped with an object. You have to remember, Ms. Collins, this happened a decade ago. DNA testing was much less sophisticated back then. The ME generally looked for sperm on a rape victim and, if he found it and the rapist was a secretor, he could identify the guilty man's blood type. That was about it."

"But in this case, the medical examiner didn't find any sperm, so we don't even have a blood type to match."

"Right."

I pulled on my chin. "Let me make sure I've got this straight," I said. "We're supposed to believe a gang of Hispanic youths went to the beach in Pacific Palisades, where they approached a party of Pali High kids. Luis Alvarez flirted with Lauren Hartley, but she rebuffed him. When Lauren left her friends to go for a walk by herself, the Hispanics gang-raped and killed her. And every last one of them wore a condom."

"Basically, that's the story." The attorney kept her eyes trained on the file folder.

"If you ask me, that whole tale sounds highly unlikely," I told her. "At the very least, this has to be loaded with reasonable doubt. So why on earth did Luis plea bargain to second degree murder instead of going to trial?"

Madeleine Raymond closed the file and placed both her hands palms down on top of it. She continued to avoid making eye contact with me. "This was one of my very first cases," she said in a voice that suddenly grew shaky. "I was right out of law school and completely overwhelmed by my new job at the PD's office." It was hard to reconcile the woman across the desk from me with the far more confident one I'd seen in court that morning. She looked vulnerable now, not at all like my fourth grade teacher. "The DA intended to file this as a capital case," she said, "and I—"

"The death penalty?" I bolted forward in my chair, stunned. "*For godsake, why?* Luis was barely eighteen, still in high school, he had no prior arrest record—"

"Politics, that's why. Look, the fact is Lauren was a rich white girl with heavy family connections. Luis was a poor Latino from downtown with no connections. There was a lot of press attention focused on this case, and the DA thought he could win."

I shook my head in disbelief, wondering if this was typical of most death penalty cases. "You're telling me the prosecutor's motivation in pushing for the death penalty against Luis Alvarez was to impress the Hartley family?"

"Not *just* that. He had several strong motivations. You're right that the entitlement factor was a major one—the victim was one of the elite, while the accused was an outsider. The DA wanted to look tough on crime, particularly violent crime in a good neighborhood like the Palisades, a part of town where people vote and have the money to make fat campaign contributions. Plus the prosecutor was miffed that Luis refused to name his accomplices—he didn't want the public thinking there were other rapist-murderers still at large. And he also wanted to wrap up this case in a hurry, to get it out of the newspapers and off the six o'clock news. If he got a quick conviction, he could move on."

"So he offered Luis a plea bargain."

"Eventually. The prosecution's first ploy was to offer the kid a break on his sentence if he would name names."

"But Luis didn't have anybody to name."

"If you believe his story."

"You didn't?"

Raymond chewed her lower lip. "I honestly don't know what I believed. I was so green I didn't know which end was up half the time. Most of the people I represented actually were guilty of the crimes they'd been charged with. My job was to get them the lightest sentence possible, which almost always meant pleading them out to a lesser charge. And I also had to handle each case as fast as humanly possible, because there'd be a dozen new files landing on my desk the next day.

"So when the DA offered us a deal to plead to second degree murder, I—I guess I urged Luis to take it. I remember telling him we'd probably lose if we went to trial, and he'd end up on death row. At the time, I honestly felt this was the kind of case where juries almost always sentence the defendant to death—privileged white victim, destitute minority defendant, the typical scenario."

"So poor Luis must have been scared enough of dying that he took the deal."

"Or else he really was guilty of the crime." Raymond picked up the file. "Look, I'm not saying there isn't enough reasonable doubt here to get the kid off." She slid the file into her desk drawer. "If Luis had Gerry Spence or Johnnie Cochrane representing him instead of me, he'd probably be a free man today. Hell, if *I* took his case today, instead of when I was a wet-behind-the-ears beginner, I'd play it completely different, too. Still, none of this proves Luis is not guilty of the rape and murder of Lauren Hartley."

"Well, it certainly doesn't prove that he *is,*" I said.

"No," Madeleine Raymond reluctantly agreed. "I have to admit it's possible Luis Alvarez is completely innocent."

Instead of taking the Santa Monica freeway to Pacific Coast Highway to get home, I drove west on Wilshire to Brentwood and cut north across Barrington to Sunset Boulevard, using the extra driving time to replay my meeting with Madeleine Raymond in my mind. By the time I turned into the driveway, maneuvered around the garbage can ready at the curb for tomorrow's pickup, and parked the Mercedes in its usual spot, I felt fairly certain that Luis

Alvarez had spent nearly a decade in prison for a crime he didn't commit. A rape and murder I felt increasingly certain was the dirty work of the Palisades Playboys.

What I hadn't figured out, however, was how I could possibly prove my suspicions. More pertinent to my original task, I had no idea what, if anything, that long-ago miscarriage of justice had to do with the deaths of Shane King and Tiffany Novotny.

My briefcase in my hand, I climbed out of my car and locked it. I glanced at the main house and noticed the kitchen light was still on. I could see Uncle Teddy's slender shadow moving behind the curtains. He was on another of his nighttime baking binges, I figured—whipping up more irresistible calories that would further sabotage my diet. Why hadn't I inherited his eat-and-stay-thin genes? If I didn't get back into my own digs soon, away from the constant temptation of Teddy's cooking, I'd undoubtedly end up the size of Camryn Manheim.

There also was a light coming from behind the fence that surrounded the backyard. Was the disaster cleanup crew still working? I opened the gate and walked around the pool. Its water drained by the cleaners, the pool now was nothing more than a big concrete hole in the ground. As soon as the filtering system was cleaned and repaired, it could be refilled and I could resume swimming my daily laps. I really missed my regular exercise—I'd felt stiff and sluggish all day.

The light I'd spotted was coming from the guesthouse, yet the front door was securely locked. I unlocked it and stepped inside, nearly knocking over a can of paint standing in the entryway.

"Hello!" I called, stepping around the paint. "Anybody here?" It was as quiet as a tomb. I quickly checked the kitchen and bedroom, but the place was deserted. Apparently the painter had forgotten to turn off the ceiling light in the hallway when he'd finished work for the day.

I saw that the soiled carpet had been removed and all the furniture that had survived the vandals now was crowded into the middle of the rooms and covered with tarps. Most of the living room already sported a new coat of creamy white paint. With luck, I thought, the painting would be finished and new carpet would be laid by the end of the week. I could move back into my own little place by Saturday.

I turned off the hall light and relocked the front door on my way out. I didn't have to decide what to do about Luis Alvarez, or figure out what his conviction might have to do with Shane and Tiffany tonight, I told myself. Surely my thoughts would be clearer tomorrow, after I'd had a nice, relaxing bath and a restful night's sleep.

I walked along the path at the edge of the pool and, as I approached the backdoor of the main house, I heard the unmistakable crash of breaking glass from the direction of the driveway.

Uncle Teddy! In my mind's eyes, I saw the old man trip and fall as he carried his recycle bin full of empty bottles and jars to the curb. I'd told him a thousand times to wait and let me do that weekly chore for him, warning that he could fall and break a hip or worse, but he was just too damned stubborn to listen. Now exactly what I'd feared had happened!

I dropped my briefcase on the grass, ran to the fence, yanked open the gate, and sprinted out into the driveway, expecting to see Teddy lying prone and bloody in a pile of broken glass. Instead, my gaze focused on the undisturbed garbage can at the curb, I sensed more than actually saw a quick movement near my car.

I pivoted around just in time to see that the side window of the Mercedes had been shattered.

"Hey!" I managed to utter an instant before a dark figure swung something long and dark at my head. I started to step back and raise my hands in self-defense, but I was too slow.

The weapon connected with its target. I felt a quick pain radiate through my skull. My knees buckled and I started to fall.

Before I reached the pavement, my world faded to black.

10

A clanging electric bell assaulted my ears, yanking me from the depths of sleep. I felt something grip my shoulder as sirens joined the piercing cacophony. *Leave me alone!* I wanted to scream, but my voice wouldn't work. *Let me sleep!*

Mercifully, the ear-splitting noise finally ceased and I felt myself starting to slip backward toward peace.

"Quinn! Quinn! Wake up!"

Why wouldn't they leave me alone?

"Wake up, sweetheart, please wake up!"

As I drifted upward toward consciousness a second time, I recognized naked fear in my uncle's shaking voice. I forced my eyelids open a crack just as the paramedic's van rounded the corner and screeched to a halt behind my Mercedes. The pain in my head was blinding. I closed my eyes again, shutting out the pulsating lights of the emergency vehicles.

"Move back, please, sir. We need room to check her out." It was a young woman's voice I heard.

I felt competent, reassuring hands probe my body for broken bones, take my blood pressure, examine the wound on my head.

"I hurt," I gasped. "God, I hurt!"

In the background, I heard Uncle Teddy explaining to the cops how he'd looked out his kitchen window, then triggered his burglar alarm, which apparently had scared off my attackers.

"There were two guys, dressed all in black," he said,

sounding breathless. “I heard glass breaking and looked out the window, that one right there. Next thing I knew, the tall one swung this crowbar he had in his hand and hit my Quinnie in the—in the—” His voice broke. “She—she’s going to be all right, isn’t she?”

“She has a nasty head wound, sir,” the woman paramedic told him. “We’ll have to take her to the hospital, get some X-rays. But I don’t see any other damage. I’m sure she’ll be just fine.”

The next thing I knew, I’d been rolled onto a gurney and was speeding toward the nearest emergency room. Uncle Teddy sat beside me in the back of the ambulance, stroking my shoulder over and over like a talisman, his dear wrinkled face a study in worry.

Periodically, I forced my eyes open, just to reassure him I was still alive. But every time I did, my head hurt worse, so I tried to keep my eyes shut tight for most of the journey.

At the hospital, after reading my X-rays, the ER doctor announced my diagnosis—a mild concussion with laceration. He put seven stitches into the side of my scalp to close the wound, handed me a bottle of pain pills with instructions printed on the label, ordered me to get plenty of rest, and told Uncle Teddy to call a cab to take us home.

Apparently my insurance didn’t allow me to actually be admitted into the hospital. Except for having my stitches removed by my private physician in a week’s time, I was now officially on my own.

The next morning, I dragged myself out of bed when I could no longer stand lying there doing nothing. My head still throbbed, despite the pain pills I’d popped during the night.

The medication alleviated the pain in my head, but it

made me feel nauseous, too. The blueberry muffin Teddy forced me to choke down for breakfast did little to alleviate that part of my agony. The best thing I could do, I decided, was find something to take my mind off my physical misery.

So I walked outside, careful to hold my aching head steady as I walked, and took a look at my damaged Mercedes. Teddy had already swept up the broken glass beneath the shattered side window, but I saw a smear of red blood on the driveway where I'd fallen. Forcing down the bile that rose in my throat, I averted my eyes and focused my attention on the car.

The glove box stood open, its innocuous contents—gasoline and car repair receipts, a pack of gum, a street map of Western L.A., a miniature flashlight—scattered across the passenger seat. The rear bench seat had been forced upward, exposing springs and years of accumulated dust beneath it. The trunk had been pried open, too, leaving a nasty ridge along the edge of the lid. I could see it would have to be pounded out and probably repainted as well.

Yet the new stereo system I'd installed last year was still intact and, strangely enough, nothing else seemed to be missing, either. If its hubcaps hadn't been still in place, I might have suspected my poor old car had survived a search by an overzealous DEA agent looking for a smuggler's stash of cocaine.

I made a mental note to call my insurance company.

Halfway back to the house, the connection I'd been missing all along finally occurred to me. My car hadn't been targeted by thieves any more than my house had. The vandalism was simply a cover for someone searching for something they believed I possessed.

Not a DEA agent, of course. I had no stash of cocaine or

anything else illicit. No, this had to be something else. But what?

I walked into the house via the backyard and backdoor, retrieving my discarded briefcase along the way. The leather was damp from the early morning fog, but otherwise the briefcase was untouched. There was nothing inside it that would be of use to anyone but me, anyway, just my reporter's notebook, my tape recorder, my day planner, my address book.

Teddy was flitting around the kitchen nervously as I entered. "Don't even think about going to work," he told me. "I called and told Harry what happened to you and he said he didn't want to see your face around the office for at least the rest of the week."

"Harry doesn't want to see my face around work for the rest of his life," I mumbled, pulling one of the chairs away from the kitchen table and slumping down into it. My business partner was certain to cite my latest misadventure as further evidence that I didn't know when to butt out of things that were none of my business.

"That's not true and you know it. The *Hollywood Star* wouldn't even exist if it weren't for you, Quinn."

What Teddy said was technically true—the proceeds from the sale of my house had pulled the newspaper back from the brink of bankruptcy—but I'd rather think it was my reporting and writing skills that were keeping the *Star* afloat than my life's savings. "You try telling Harry how indispensable I am," I moaned, holding my head in my hands. "He gets tired of hearing it from me."

"How about I make you some coffee?" Teddy reached for the coffee pot.

He obviously was eager to help, but his hovering was starting to drive me crazy. "What I'd really like," I told him, "is the use of your desk and phone."

He shot me a disapproving look. "You're not going to try to work today, I hope. The doctor said you needed to rest, Quinnie."

"I'll try my very best not to do any thinking," I shot back, then instantly regretted my sarcasm. The poor man was obviously worried about me and trying to look out for my interests as best he knew how. "Sorry, Teddy. I don't mean to snap at you. I just need to make a couple of phone calls, that's all. And I'll go crazy if I have to do nothing but lie around all day. I promise not to do anything strenuous."

Teddy considered the options for a moment. "Well, okay, then. How about we set you up on the living room sofa? I'll bring the portable phone in there. That way, you can lie down while you make your calls."

I agreed out of sheer frustration. If I could manage to keep Teddy from eavesdropping on my conversations, I told myself, I might be able to accomplish something after all.

My first call was to Lucy, asking her to let me know about any messages for me that might come into the office today. She gushed over me and last night's misadventure almost as much as Uncle Teddy had. Two mother hens were almost more than I could stomach. When she offered to pick up some chicken soup from Kantor's on her lunch hour and deliver it to me here at home, I almost lost it.

"Thanks, Lucy, but I've already got Uncle Teddy playing nursemaid," I told her, hoping I didn't sound too ungrateful. Instead, I gave her a couple of tasks to do and asked her to call me back as soon as she had the results.

I called Peter King next.

"I was wondering if I'd ever hear from you again," he snapped as soon as he recognized my voice. "I've been trying to call you, but you haven't been answering your phone."

I was in no mood. "Look, Peter, somebody tried to bash my head in last night because of you, so lose the attitude, huh?" I told him about my last few days, describing in detail the damage to my guesthouse, my car, and my head.

His demeanor changed instantly. "Jesus, Quinn, I'm sorry. You really think this has something to do with Shane?"

"I'm almost positive. Look, we need to talk."

"I'm listening."

"I mean in person." What I had to say shouldn't be said over the phone. "I'm grounded for at least the rest of today. How about you come over to Teddy's place this afternoon?" If Peter was at home this late in the morning, I knew full well he was out of work and had time on his hands.

"Two o'clock okay?"

"See you then." As soon as I hung up, the phone rang. It was Lucy.

"Detective Lewis says to tell you he's sorry to hear about what happened," she told me.

"That's nice," I said, feeling irrationally impatient with how sorry everybody felt for me. "Did he have that report I need?"

"Faxed it right over."

Now maybe we'd get somewhere. If only my fax machine in the guesthouse hadn't been trashed, I'd have had her fax it to me here. Instead, I was forced to ask her what it said.

"I'm not sure, exactly. It's pretty complicated, written in medical jargon," she said, "all this stuff about the weight of that poor boy's liver and the size of his heart. What did they do, take him apart piece by piece?"

"Pretty much, yes. That's what happens when they do an autopsy."

"How horribly gory."

"Just skip over all that stuff, Lucy, find the paragraph that states the cause of death. It'll be toward the end. Read me that much, will you?"

There was a long pause on the line. "Here it is," she said, finally. "The cause of death is toxic heroin ingestion. That's what you're looking for, right?"

"Right. Confirms Tracy's guess at the scene. Is there any evidence of damage to Shane's skull?" After my own experience, I wondered whether somebody had knocked the kid unconscious before injecting the heroin into his vein.

"I don't see anything like that."

It had probably been a stupid question. Tracy was nobody's fool. He would have noticed a head wound like the one I was sporting if there'd been one.

"See if there's a section noting the contents of the stomach, Lucy."

"Right. It says here the victim's stomach was empty except for partially digested beer and some popcorn."

Beer. Could Shane have been drunk, perhaps passed out, when his murderer shot him up with heroin? "What's his blood alcohol level?"

"Point zero two."

Nowhere near drunk. "Any other drugs present?"

"It talks about something called flu—flunitrazepam. Is that a drug?"

"Sounds like one to me. How do you spell it?" I wrote down the word as Lucy spelled it for me. I cursed myself for not having taken the time to replace my trashed home computer. Now I wouldn't be able to use the Internet to find out what sort of drug this was. For all I knew, it could be anything from a vitamin pill to rat poison. "Thanks, Lucy. This is a big help."

"I'm still waiting on that other report you asked for," she said. "I'll call you as soon as it comes in."

After I hung up, I called the reference librarian at Santa Monica Library and asked her to look up flunitrazepam in the *Physicians Desk Reference*, but she couldn't find it listed. Now my interest was really piqued. I asked her to see if she could find any mention of it on the net and call me back as soon as possible.

I got Tracy Lewis' voice mail when I phoned his office. He must have left right after faxing Shane's autopsy report to Lucy. If I were paranoid, I might think he was avoiding me, afraid I'd question him about this flunitrazepam stuff and force him to rethink his opinion that Shane King's death was an accidental OD. I left him a message.

A few minutes later, the librarian called back. "I found some information about flunitrazepam on the Haight Ashbury Free Clinic's website," she said. "It's a sleeping pill marketed in Mexico, South America, Europe and Asia."

"Any illegal street use here?" I asked.

"Right," she said. "Let me read you this part, 'It has been used by heroin addicts as an enhancer for low-quality heroin, and in combination with cocaine to moderate the effects of a binge.' The Clinic's report goes on to say, 'The most common pattern is episodic use by teenagers and young adults as an alcohol extender and disinhibitory agent, most often in combination with beer.' "

I thought for a moment. Maybe Tracy had been right after all. If Shane was a heroin user, could be he'd combined his drug of choice with flunitrazepam, thinking he was using low-quality heroin instead of the high-quality stuff he'd really injected. "Sounds like this stuff is legal outside the U.S.," I told the librarian. "Does the report mention a brand name?"

She gave it to me. I wrote down a far more familiar word. "Thanks, you've been a great help," I told her. As I hung up the phone, a new theory began to take shape in my mind.

At two o'clock, a disapproving Uncle Teddy ushered Peter King into his living room. "Quinn's supposed to be resting," he said to both of us.

Peter was carrying a bouquet of bearded irises. I was touched that he'd remember my favorite flowers after all these years, and I hoped he wouldn't be sorry he'd gone to the trouble of finding them once he'd heard what I had to say.

"How lovely," I said. "Thank you, Peter. That's really thoughtful." I turned to Teddy. "Would you mind finding a vase for these, please, Teddy?"

His lips pursed in silent condemnation, Teddy took the flowers and carried them toward the kitchen.

Peter sat in a chair opposite the sofa. We spent a few minutes making small talk and I was chagrined to realize I felt embarrassed to have my former lover see me at my least attractive—no makeup, a bandage plastered on my head, my hair bedraggled, looking tired and drained. The fact that my trying to help him out was precisely what had put me in this shape in the first place didn't seem to matter. Old habits die hard, I guess.

It was time we got down to business. "Did your son Rhett keep a diary or anything like that?" I asked.

"Rhett? I guess he had a few journals he liked to write in," Peter said. "Why?"

I ignored his question. "Did you read those journals? I

mean after he died, of course."

"Just the last one, that's all." Peter stared down at his hands. They were shaking slightly. "I suppose I wanted to reassure myself Rhett didn't . . ."

"Commit suicide?"

Peter's gaze shot upward again and he stared at me. "You always did cut right to the heart of things, didn't you, Quinn?"

I couldn't argue that point. "Were there a lot of these journals?"

"Quite a few, I think. Rhett started writing them during his sophomore year. If I remember right, it was some sort of English class assignment in the beginning, but for some reason it appealed to him and he kept it up."

It probably served as an amateur form of psychotherapy for a sensitive—or guilty—young man, I figured. "You didn't read all his journals, though, right?"

Peter shook his head. Suddenly he looked as tired and worn out as I felt. "No, no I didn't. I never liked invading my son's privacy, even after—Hey, what's all this about, anyway? Why are you asking me about Rhett? I asked you to look into Shane's death, not his brother's."

I took a breath and hoped for the best. "I think both Shane and his girlfriend were killed because they knew too much about something," I told Peter, "and I think that something is connected to both Rhett and the death of Lauren Hartley." Peter started to argue, but I held up my hand in protest. "Just bear with me a minute here, please, and I'll explain everything. Do you know where Rhett's journals are now?"

Peter shook his head. "He left everything he owned to his brother. I suppose Shane must have kept them, unless he threw them out when he moved to the beach house."

I felt positive Shane hadn't discarded his brother's journals, that he'd hidden them somewhere he thought they'd be safe. "Are you telling me Rhett had a will?" I asked Peter. That seemed a bit strange for a twenty-year-old, unless he'd expected to die.

"Just a simple hand-written sort of thing, plus a life insurance policy he bought. Listed his brother as his beneficiary on that, too. Veronica and I thought the insurance money would help pay for Shane's college education, but things didn't work out quite the way we planned."

My guess was that Shane found an easier way than struggling through four years of college to get what he wanted out of life. "Shane didn't do all that well in college, did he?" I'd learned that much from my interview with the young movie mogul.

"I think this is just about enough, Quinn," Peter said, straightening his spine. "Tell me what you're getting at."

"Like I told you, Peter, I think Shane and Tiffany were murdered because they found out who raped and murdered Lauren Hartley . . . and it was not the young man who's been sitting in prison all these years, convicted and sentenced for that crime."

"But who—"

Without revealing my source, I told Peter all about the Palisades Playboys and the scorecards they'd kept rating their sexual escapades.

He bristled. "What does that bunch of horny losers have to do with my sons?"

"Doesn't sound like Rhett was a member of the Palisades Playboys, but he certainly knew about them. They were his neighbors, his buddies. And he and his girlfriend, Julia Jackson, were at the beach party the night Lauren was attacked and killed. Julia told me she had too much to drink and passed out. She thought Rhett did, too." I locked onto Peter's gaze. "I think Rhett woke up long before Julia did."

Peter stared back at me, his eyes dark with confusion. "What are you trying to tell me?"

"I think the Palisades Playboys raped Lauren Hartley. They'd all been drinking and doing drugs at the party. Lauren was a virgin, and virgins were their favorite target. I believe things got out of hand after Julia passed out, maybe the boys egged each other on. They might have convinced themselves Lauren wanted to have sex with them, or maybe they just didn't give a damn *what* she wanted. Could be she struggled and, while trying to hold her down, they accidentally suffocated her." Or maybe they murdered her on purpose to keep her from charging them with rape, but I didn't verbalize that thought.

"However it happened," I said, "Lauren ended up dead and the Palisades Playboys had to find a way to cover their asses. That's where their classmate, Luis Alvarez, came in. They'd seen him on the beach earlier in the evening. He was a Chicano, one of the disadvantaged kids bused into Pali High from the inner city, a boy these rich, privileged kids felt infinitely superior to. It was easy enough for them to pin their crime on Luis."

Peter was growing pale. "You still haven't said what any of this has to do with my sons."

"Rhett backed up his buddies' version of events with the police, Peter. You must remember that much. I don't know whether he actually saw the rape, or if the others told him about it afterward and asked him to corroborate their story, or even if he—"

"Rhett was no rapist!" Peter shouted. He lunged forward, his fists clenched. "And he sure as hell was no murderer!"

"I never said he was, Peter. Calm down. All I said was Rhett seems to have helped frame an innocent classmate for something his friends did. I think that's what tore him apart afterward, what started him on hard drugs. He was trying to ignore his conscience."

"You have no proof of any of this, no proof at all."

I took a deep breath and touched a finger to my temple. My head was starting to throb again. "You're right, I don't, not without Rhett's journals, and I don't know where they are." Obviously somebody thought I had them, however. That was the only explanation I could think of for the break-ins. "Look at the circumstantial evidence here, though, Peter. How do you think Shane got that big job at Calistoga Pictures? It certainly wasn't because he knew so much about the film business."

"I—I guess I just figured it was connections. His mother probably knew somebody at Calistoga, he was in the right place at the right time, you know how things work in this town."

"How about this?" I asked. "Let's suppose Shane read all of Rhett's journals and he found some information there he could use. What if he went to Troy Kellerman and demanded to be paid off to keep his mouth shut about the Palisades Playboys and Lauren's murder? What if Kellerman's father gave Shane the job at Calistoga Pictures as a payoff, a way to transfer money to him while getting the production company to foot the bill?"

"You're telling me Shane was blackmailing these people?"

I nodded slowly.

Peter shot to his feet, his face crimson. "I never should have asked for your help. Jesus, Quinn, you're accusing Shane of being a blackmailer and Rhett, at the very least, of being an accomplice to rape and murder."

"I guess I am."

"With friends like you, I—Fuck you, Quinn Collins! Forget I ever asked you to do anything for me. Forget about your half-assed theory. I want you to leave my family alone!" He stalked out of the room. I heard the front door slam.

A minute or two later, Teddy stuck his head around the corner. "Was that the front door I heard? Is Peter gone?"

"Apparently so," I said, feeling like my old lover had just slapped me across the face.

"Well, I'm certainly glad he listened to me and didn't stay so long he wore you out," Teddy said with a self-satisfied smile on his face. "Do try to get some rest now, Quinnie. You look like you could use it."

Where were Rhett King's journals? As I lay on my uncle's sofa, feeling depressed and unable to nap, I went over all the possibilities I could think of. Obviously Rhett's notes weren't at Shane's beach house. Whoever'd killed him had had all night to search that place after Shane was dead.

Yet the killer must have thought it possible he'd missed them. Because I was the one who'd discovered Shane's dead body, the killer—or, more likely, killers—must have thought I'd found the journals and taken them away with me.

Or maybe they'd come after me for a different reason, because I'd been questioning Tiffany. Did the killers suspect that Shane gave Tiffany the journals and she later passed them on to me?

I mused for a while about the beautiful young Tiffany. Shane's killers might have thought she had the evidence against them simply because she was Shane's obsession and they hadn't found what they needed at Shane's house. But if I had to bet, I'd say something more had come into play here.

Tiffany was nothing if not an opportunist. My guess was she knew all about Shane's scam, possibly even had possession of the damning journals. But, after Shane was murdered, rather than go to the police with the evidence, I was willing to bet she was the kind of girl who would try to blackmail the killers herself.

That would explain Tiffany's belief that she'd suddenly landed the lead female role in a new movie. Her goal in life hadn't been money alone, it had been fame, and she probably thought the Palisades Playboys had the power to make her both rich and famous. After Shane died and with the journals in her possession, she could have convinced herself she had the perfect catalyst to launch her career.

But instead of getting her the promised movie role, it looked like the Palisades Playboys had duped her, luring her to her death off a Big Sur cliff.

Yet the killers still didn't have Rhett's journals. If they'd recovered them from Tiffany, either here in town or in Big Sur, they'd never have invaded my guesthouse, my office, even my car, looking for them.

I pushed myself up into a sitting position on the sofa and reached for the telephone. Luckily, I caught Tiffany's aunt Emma at home and she remembered me. After expressing my condolences about the loss of her niece, I described what I was looking for. I didn't tell her why.

"Wouldn't know about no set of books like that," she said, sounding as if she was about to cry. "Ralph and me, we drove back down from Salinas after Tiffany's funeral and—and—"

"And what?"

"We get back home here and what do you think we find? Somebody broke in while we were away, that's what. Can you believe some people? Ain't enough we got a death in the family, that we lost our wonderful little Tiffany so young. Now we gotta—we gotta deal with some damn thief, too."

I did my best to soothe Mrs. Novotny, yet get off the phone as quickly as possible. I now felt certain Tiffany hadn't hidden Rhett's journals at her aunt and uncle's house. If they'd been there, the killers wouldn't have been breaking into my car last night, and I wouldn't be sitting here on my uncle's sofa with a fresh row of stitches in my scalp.

The only other place I figured Tiffany might have hidden the journals was at her parents' house on the farm. The farm was also the last place the young woman had been before her death.

Shirley Novotny answered her phone on the sixth ring. "Sorry, I was out in the garden," she said after I identified myself. She sounded breathless. "Thought I'd better prune back those rose bushes while I had a free hour. You know how it is—gardening helps keep my mind off things."

We exchanged a few pleasantries.

"Thanks a lot for sending up that nice obituary notice you wrote about Tiffany," she told me. "That was real good of you."

"You're certainly welcome. Tiffany was a very promising young actress, and I'm sure she would have been a valuable addition to our industry," I lied. "It'll appear in this week's edition of the *Star.*"

After I explained what I was looking for, Shirley told me, "Haven't seen anything like that. I'm positive there's no stack of diaries or journals here. Tiffany came home with nothing but her suitcase, and she took it with her again when she left for the movie set. Nothing in her room now but stuff left from before she moved down to L.A."

"And nobody's tried to break into your house?" I asked.

There was a long pause. "No, not ours, but—"

"But what?"

"The Olsons, Barbara and Stuart, up at the main house? Somebody broke in their place. When we were all at church for Tiffany's funeral."

"I've heard burglars sometimes read funeral notices in the newspaper, Shirley, that they choose the exact time of the funeral to break in because they know that's when the family will be away," I told her. "Probably thought you lived in the big house."

"Think so?"

I did, but I didn't explain to Shirley why I was so certain. I could think of no good reason to tell a grieving mother her daughter had been murdered, or why, not before I had absolute proof of my theory.

"Will you do me a small favor?" I asked her.

"Sure, if I can. You were awful good to my little girl."

"Just take one more good look through the house, especially in Tiffany's bedroom, and see if there's anything, anything at all that could be even a little part of Rhett King's journals. It might be nothing more than a few pages torn out, something small enough to slip under a mattress or into the bottom of a dresser drawer."

"That sounds awful sinister. Why on earth would Tiff want to hide somebody else's diary that way?"

"I'll explain everything later, Shirley," I promised. "For now, just see if you can find anything like that, okay? I'll call you back tomorrow."

She agreed.

I spent another half hour in the living room, making notes, then phoned the office.

"Hey, Quinn, I was just going to call you," Lucy said. "How do you feel?"

"Irritable, and my head still hurts like hell," I said. "But enough of my medical history. Did you get those e-mail addresses I wanted?"

"Of course." I copied them down as Lucy read them to me.

"Anything happening?" I asked her.

"That report you wanted from Monterey County finally came in. I tell you, I'm starting to feel like I'm stuck in an episode of 'Quincy' around here."

The autopsy report on Tiffany Novotny. I picked up my notebook and pen. "Shoot," I said.

"Questionable choice of words, Quinn."

"Why? Was the girl shot?"

"No, of course she wasn't shot. She drove off a cliff, for heaven's sake. It's just that all this blood and gore—Oh, forget it."

"What's listed as the official cause of death?" I asked, cutting to the chase.

"A whole bunch of horrible-sounding injuries consistent with the car crash. That poor girl. Sure hope she died right away, that she didn't have to suffer too much."

"I'm sure she didn't suffer, Lucy." So much for the idea that Tiffany was already dead before her car went off the mountainside. "What about the toxicology screen? What does that say?"

"Let me see if I can find that part." I heard papers rustling before Lucy's voice came back on the line. "This sounds like it here. Hey, this is a little weird."

"What's weird?"

"Isn't this the same drug Shane King was taking? Flu—fluni—flunitrazepam. Don't know if I'm pronouncing that name right."

Bingo! So that's how they did it. "Doesn't matter, Lucy. I've got it. It's the same drug all right, and you're a genius. Thank you!"

"Hey, all I did was take a piece of paper off the fax machine and read it to you."

When I hung up the telephone, I knew exactly how Shane King and Tiffany Novotny had been killed, and I knew why.

All I needed now was to figure out how I could prove what I already knew . . . before the killers decided that I, like Shane and Tiffany, had become a liability they had to eliminate.

11

By the next morning, I was bored silly sitting around the house, doing nothing but recuperating from my head wound. I had to wonder how a Type A like me would ever make it through a really long illness; I'd probably die of boredom long before cancer or heart disease ever managed to take me out.

By the time I finished my second cup of coffee, the new laptop and portable printer I'd ordered had been delivered by the local computer store. I'd needed a new computer anyway, I told myself, and a laptop would be much more convenient than my desktop model, the one that had ended up in the bottom of the swimming pool.

I was back in business, a fact that lifted my spirits immensely.

Lucky for me, today was Uncle Teddy's shopping day. He always coupled his weekly visit to the Farmer's Market with a lunch date with an old friend. Then, he'd visit the local fish market and grocery store on his way home. Today, as he made out his shopping lists, he fussed over me, promising to stay home instead and take care of me, if I'd just say the word.

The only word I really had to say to him was, *"Out!"* Well, okay, I said it a lot more gently than that, but after he left, I let out a huge sigh of relief. I was grateful to be free of the old man's worried face hovering over me for at least a few hours.

I did not object, however, when Teddy insisted on setting the house's security alarm system as he departed, empty shopping bags in hand. Stupid I'm not.

As soon as I saw Teddy's car pull out of the driveway, I phoned Shirley Novotny.

"I looked everywhere," she told me, "but I didn't find anything like what you described."

I felt a strong pang of disappointment, wondering if I'd ever locate Rhett King's journals.

"I did find one strange thing, though," Shirley said.

"What's that?"

"There was a key on the floor under Tiffany's bed."

"What kind of key?"

"Silver, smaller than a door key or a car key. It's got a little gold chain attached, with a plastic disk on it. The disk has a number printed on one side, but nothing else. I've never seen it before, and I must have vacuumed under that bed a thousand times."

My pulse quickened. "Do you happen to know where Tiffany did her banking?" I asked.

"Not off hand, but probably Emma and Oscar would. Most likely one of the banks near their house in Palms. Why?"

"That key sounds like it goes to a safety deposit box," I told her. My morale rocketed out of the cellar. It might take a little leg work to locate and retrieve them, but I now felt sure Rhett's journals were well within reach.

The first story I wrote on my new computer took me a bit less than two hours to complete. That was fast for me, given its length and detail, but I'd been writing and re-writing it in my head all night. I checked over what I'd written, then added a headline—"Decade-Old Rape, 3 Murders Linked to Industry Powerbrokers." The headline was a bit wordy, I had to admit, and not entirely accurate—not everybody in my story was technically an industry power-broker. But what I'd written would not be published in its present form, anyway.

I printed out my story and read the hard copy. I'd included every aspect of the Palisades Playboys story, starting with Lauren Hartley's murder and ending with Tiffany Novotny's. I identified the suspects by name and occupation, citing strong evidence implicating Troy Kellerman, Joseph Taliaferro, and Stevenson Brooks in rape and multiple murder. My story stated that Parker Kellerman was suspected of both using Calistoga Pictures' funds to pay blackmail demands and taking part in a cover-up of his son's more serious crimes.

I also added a few details I knew I couldn't prove, at least not yet—that a new DNA test was expected to prove Luis Alvarez had been sent to prison for a crime the Palisades Playboys had committed, and that Rhett King's newly-discovered journals described in great detail both the original crime and the plan that set up Luis as the scapegoat. I took a bit of license with these portions because I planned to edit this piece many times before it appeared in the *Star.* The DNA evidence wasn't real, at least as far as I knew, but I had strong hope that Tiffany's safety deposit box really contained Rhett's incriminating journals. In the meantime, if my allegations gave the guilty a stronger case of heartburn, so much the better.

I had a brief bout with heartburn myself, as I read my story for the umpteenth time. Did I really want to do this? I knew full well that Hollywood had a long history of punishing whistleblowers. I'm old enough to remember what happened to actor Cliff Robertson when he turned in studio executive David Begelman, the man who'd used Robertson's name to steal from studio coffers. Robertson hadn't been able to get work for years. Instead of rewarding the innocent actor for his bravery, Hollywood had circled its wagons to protect the guilty outlaw.

Still, I reminded myself, I couldn't forget I was my father's daughter. My dad hadn't buckled when the communist-hunting McCarthyites came after him and his friends. He'd done the right thing, chosen the strict moral course, knowing it could cost him his career. And, of course, it did.

The current circumstances were far more serious. This time, people had been murdered. How could I possibly *not* do whatever it took to reveal the truth? If it cost me my career, so be it—I didn't have the stomach to help cover up this kind of crime merely to save my job.

Not even to save the *Hollywood Star.*

My first move was to leave a detailed phone message for Detective Tracy Lewis, telling him it was an emergency and begging him to call me back as quickly as he could.

Then I hooked up my new laptop to Uncle Teddy's telephone line, dialed up my Internet connection, squared my shoulders and, using the cyber-addresses Lucy'd obtained for me, began to e-mail copies of my story. I sent one each to both Kellermans, Brooks, and Taliaferro, attaching notes asking them to tell me their side of the story, which I promised to include in my article. I listed my cell phone number and told them I was ready to go to press without their comments if I'd received no response by the end of the day.

After I'd sent the last of the e-mails, I sat back and waited for the phone to ring.

Sitting on the patio at the Surfside Cafe, nervously waiting for the people I'd arranged to meet, I adjusted my sun hat for the third or fourth time. My healing head wound itched almost unbearably in the warm morning sunshine, but I'd worn the hat to hide the stitches still in my scalp. As long as I kept it on, I hoped to look normal, not like the recent invalid I actually was.

I gazed past the three-foot-high fence surrounding the patio and over the Venice Beach boardwalk, which occupied the space between the cafe and a broad stretch of sand leading to the Pacific's shoreline. I counted half a dozen homeless men, a couple of roller skaters, a matched pair of sun-bronzed weightlifters, three old men sitting on a bench, a selection of sunbathers and people walking their dogs.

I did not see Tracy Lewis. I checked the time; it was almost ten. Where the hell was he?

Tracy hadn't called me back last night until well after I'd already arranged what he called my "harebrained scheme." He'd been busy on a stakeout, he told me, not sounding the least bit apologetic for keeping me waiting. Still, he'd listened to my entire story and reluctantly agreed to help me.

"Why the hell did you set this thing up in Venice?" he griped after finally admitting I might actually be right that Shane King had been murdered.

"Because these are cold-blooded killers, Tracy," I said. "I want to see them in full public view, somewhere I can make a fast exit if things start to go south." Somewhere there would be enough witnesses around that these guys would be unlikely to try adding me to their list of murder victims. "The Surfside popped into my mind as the perfect place for safety."

"And I suppose there's nothing equivalent in the district where I actually work? Jesus, Quinn, Venice is the L.A.P.D.'s jurisdiction, not the Sheriff's. You should know that. Now if I'm going to give you any protection, I'm gonna have to lean on the L.A. cops for backup."

Frankly, that didn't seem like a bad thing to me, not when I would be meeting with three men who clearly wanted to put my neck in a noose. What was the point of Tracy's playing the Lone Ranger? But what I said to him was, "Sorry, guess I wasn't thinking."

"For a change."

"Hey, I almost got my head bashed in the other night, okay? I'm lucky I can think at all. Cut me a little slack here, will you?"

After he cooled off, Tracy listened to what I'd planned for my little get-together with Joseph Taliaferro and the Kellermans. The three of them had reacted quickly and angrily to my e-mailed expose. When they called me, I arranged to meet them at the Surfside Cafe at ten this morning, promising I would hear their side of the story in a joint interview session. I also implied there might be a way I could be convinced to hold off or even cancel publication of my story.

I got no response at all from Stevenson Brooks. I figured he was handling this event in his young life the same way he'd handled other tensions over the past few years—by getting zonked out of his mind.

At ten o'clock sharp, I saw the Kellermans stroll out of the main restaurant and onto the patio, heading toward my table. They were accompanied by a tall young man with dark auburn hair and a dusting of freckles across his nose. Obviously, this was Joseph Taliaferro, the only one of the Palisades Playboys I hadn't yet met. None of the three looked happy to see me.

I still didn't spot Tracy. I'd envisioned him sitting at a table here on the patio, one where he could keep an eye on whatever transpired and make me feel protected. At the very least, by now he should have been stationed somewhere nearby on the boardwalk. I didn't dare look around again. The last thing I wanted to do was tip off my interview subjects that I'd involved the cops in this morning's little gathering.

By the time we'd made our introductions and had been served the coffee and tea we ordered, the other patio tables were filling up with customers and I began to feel a bit more confident I would survive this meeting. I pulled an old portable tape recorder from my purse and set it in the middle of the table. My three companions exchanged looks as I switched it on.

"I need to make sure I get your quotes accurately," I said, forcing a smile as I slipped my hand back inside my bag for an instant. I began to speak directly into the tape recorder. "I'm at the Surfside Cafe in Venice Beach, interviewing Troy Kellerman, Parker Keller—"

"No tape recorder!" Parker Kellerman snapped at me as he reached across the table and switched off my machine.

I shrugged. "Okay, if that's the way you want it, but you'll be taking your chances that I can get your exact words down." I reached into my purse again and pulled out a reporter's notebook and pencil. "Now you all say you've read my article. Probably the easiest way for us to proceed is for each of you to give me your reactions to it. Troy, why don't you begin?"

The younger Kellerman glared at me and kept silent.

"Let's cut the bullshit, lady," his father said. "Does Harry Radner know you're trying to use the *Hollywood Star* to libel his advertisers?"

"Harry and I are business partners," I told him. "Harry doesn't tell me how to write my stories and I don't tell him how to sell ad space. Works out much better that way." How I wished that were true.

"You and Harry won't be business partners much longer if you print one word of this libelous piece of shit." Parker pulled the computer printout of my e-mailed article from the inside pocket of his suit jacket and waved it in my face. "I'll sue you and the *Hollywood Star* into oblivion."

"Look, Parker, let's get real. We all know my story isn't libelous. It might embarrass you in front of your friends and colleagues, maybe get you fired from that fancy job of yours. The three of you, plus your spaced-out buddy Steve, might well go to prison after it's published . . . for a very long time. But one thing you will *not* be doing is proving what I wrote is libelous in a court of law. Count on it."

"Bitch," Taliaferro muttered under his breath.

"I heard that, Mr. Taliaferro. Your attitude's not helping your case."

"You can't prove any of this," Troy said, the muscles of his jaw flexing. "You're just guessing."

"You wish. Rhett King's journals spell out your original crime quite explicitly. Plus they show how you and your buddies conspired to blame what you'd done on poor Luis Alvarez."

"Rhett's dead," Taliaferro said. It was obvious that fact didn't particularly bother him. "You claim you've got a bunch of journals he wrote, but you don't have a whit of proof they're his. For all anybody knows, you wrote this crap yourself."

"Go ahead, take that gamble. Rhett's dad has plenty of other correspondence from him, the school has applications he filled out, there are samples of his handwriting all over the place. We'll just let the handwriting experts decide.

"Besides, the journals are only the beginning of the evidence I used to write my story. What if I told you I'd located Steve's source for the Rohypnol you used to drug

Shane and Tiffany before you killed them?" I was improvising here, but the panicked look I saw on Troy's face confirmed I'd hit my target. "Not very inventive, fellas. Using the date rape drug? And trusting a dope-head like Steve to score it for you? You had to know he'd screw it up somehow."

Troy turned to Taliaferro. "You and your bright ideas. You should've known that asshole couldn't—"

"Shut the fuck up, Troy!" the taller man said.

"Then there are the fingerprints in Tiffany's car, and the ones in Shane's house," I said. "The private investigator I used matched them, and now they're holed away in a nice, safe place."

Parker Kellerman took a swig of his coffee and plastered an unconcerned look across his face. He looked a lot older in the harsh glare of sunlight, or maybe he just hadn't slept well last night. "So what?" he said. "Shane was a friend of my son and his buddies. Finding their fingerprints in his house doesn't mean a damn thing."

I used my straw to stir my iced tea, but I didn't sip it. I probably was being paranoid, but how could I be sure I hadn't glanced away just long enough for one of these three to slip a little Rohypnol into my drink? "Ordinarily I'd have to agree with you, Parker," I said, "but see, there's another problem. Most of Shane's house was wiped clean of fingerprints after he was murdered. Looks like you guys really went to a lot of trouble there. Except you missed a few spots and they're not the sort of places a guest in somebody's home would ordinarily be touching." I thought about telling them we'd found prints inside the cupboards, on closet shelves, that sort of thing, but figured getting too specific could only get me in trouble. "Tell you the truth, it looks like somebody searched every square inch of Shane's house, looking for, let's say, his brother's journals, something like that. And I don't suppose you figured anybody'd ever bother checking a car that ran off a Big Sur cliff for fingerprints, did you?" I added.

Troy glared at the other young man. "Jesus! You and your dumb-ass ideas."

Taliaferro glared back. "I told you to shut up, Troy."

Parker Kellerman laid his palms flat on the table and leaned toward me. "How much is it worth to you not to publish this . . . this hatchet job?" he asked. Now we were getting somewhere.

"Are you trying to bribe me, Parker?"

His face was blank of expression. "I certainly wouldn't use that word, Quinn." Oddly enough, this time he'd actually gotten my name right. Amazing what it takes to get folks to remember a picky little detail like a journalist's byline. "Let's just call this a business proposition. We're simply negotiating a deal for you to sell us all rights to your article, Rhett King's journals, your notes, whatever so-called evidence that PI of yours picked up, anything and everything you claim to have that might back up that libelous story of yours."

I held up my hand in protest. "We've already been over that, Parker. My story is *not* libelous. In case you don't remember, truth is an absolute defense to libel, and every word of what I wrote is true. You want to do business with me, disparaging my work is no way to start your negotiations."

Kellerman's eyes narrowed, but he kept his temper under control. "Sorry, Quinn. I certainly don't mean to insult you or your work. What's your asking price?"

I paused a moment, pretending to think it over. "Two million dollars," I said finally, "deposited directly into an offshore bank account." I was beginning to feel like a character in a caper movie.

"What the . . . ? You've got to be kidding!" Parker's face went pale.

"Not at all. Let's see what we've got here." I began to tick off points on my fingers. "Three murders, one gang rape, an innocent kid who's spent the last decade in prison, a little bribery, a bit of fraud and blatant misuse of Calistoga Pictures' funds. Did I forget anything? Oh yes, your alternative. After my story is published, you guys can go hire yourself some high-priced lawyers, see if you can keep your butts out of prison for the rest of your lives. By then, a couple of million dollars is going to seem cheap. You don't believe me, ask O.J. So take your choice—you can pay me now or you can pay the lawyers later."

The three exchanged glances and, once again, the senior Kellerman took the initiative. "How do we even know you've got this so-called proof?"

"I thought that was obvious—I used it to write my story. You really think I could be this on-target without plenty of documented proof?"

"I think she really does have it, Dad," Troy said. I could hear the pleading tone in his voice and see the fear on his face. What if his daddy wouldn't or couldn't bail him out of trouble one more time? "We've got to find the money to buy her off."

Joe Taliaferro shook his head in disbelief. "I don't believe you two wimps." He pushed his chair back from the table, opened his windbreaker a few inches, and pointed a finger toward his chest.

My breath caught in my throat. Underneath his jacket I spotted a shoulder holster with the black butt of a handgun resting under his left armpit. He wouldn't dare shoot me right here, in public. *Would he?*

"You're going to stand up now, Quinn," Taliaferro said calmly. "We're going to walk out of here without making any trouble. Then you're going to take us to those journals. Otherwise . . ." He tapped his finger against the gun.

Parker whipped a twenty-dollar bill out of his billfold and set it down on the table. He must have known stiffing the waitress would be a crime.

Clutching my purse in both hands, I shoved back my chair and rose slowly to my feet, trying to check my surroundings as casually as possible. Where was Tracy? He was in real danger of missing his cue. This was certainly the time for him and his L.A.P.D. buddies to take over, but where the hell were they?

As Troy moved toward me and grabbed for my arm, I swiveled around and bolted over the low fence onto the boardwalk. My shin scraped the top of one of the pickets, but I didn't fall—thank goodness for long legs. I ran north, zigzagging around roller skaters and walkers and nearly plowing down an old woman pushing a shopping cart. My sun hat flew off my head and an unleashed mutt leapt on it with a bark of delight.

As I reached the end of the block, I glanced back for an instant and spotted both Troy and Joe gaining on me. I ran full out, clutching my bag against my chest. These guys were more than a decade younger than I was and they hadn't been bashed over the head in the past few days. The smart money was definitely not on my outrunning them for long.

Now people were stopping to stare at us. I nearly collided with a huge black man in a brief day-glo orange bathing suit as he walked two leashed great Danes. The confrontation slowed me up just enough to let Joe, whose long legs made him faster than Troy, come within a few feet of me.

I darted to the side of the boardwalk and shot behind a tilted table displaying sunglasses for sale. Grabbing a hold of the side of the table, I shoved it over. Sunglasses scattered in all directions.

"Hey, lady!" the stunned vendor yelled. "What the hell?"

But my tactic bought me a little time. Taliaferro caught his toe on a leg of the toppled display, tripped, and landed hard on his knees as I fled farther down the boardwalk toward Santa Monica.

My heart pounding in my chest, I crossed the city line. There were fewer pedestrians here. Had I run in the wrong direction, putting myself in more danger?

As I struggled to catch my breath, I glanced behind me and saw Troy and Joe quickly closing in on me, two homeless men on their heels. What in the—? Almost at the end of my strength, I reached inside my purse and managed to grab my cell phone. I punched in 9-1-1 and, as the operator answered, I shoved my purse through the wrought-iron gate of the plush Sea Colony condo complex.

"Help! They're trying to kill me!" I gasped into my phone, my legs quickly turning to rubber.

But before I could give the operator my location, Troy Kellerman tackled me from behind and my phone flew out of my hand. I fell hard on my hip and elbow and skidded across the concrete. I heard a siren somewhere in the distance. *Too late for me,* I thought, as my head banged against something hard and unforgiving. I blacked out.

"Quinn? Quinn? You okay?"

I opened my eyes and slowly the face hanging above

mine came into focus. "Tracy," I murmured. "Wh—where were—?"

"Stuck in traffic on PCH. Fatality accident. Got here as fast as I could."

I was still lying on the path outside Sea Colony. My head felt like someone had pounded roofing nails through it, but apparently my loss of consciousness was brief.

"Sorry," Tracy said sheepishly. "But my buddies took good care of you, right?"

Sure, that's why I'd probably never walk again, I thought, my hip throbbing nearly as much as my head. "What buddies?"

Tracy slid his beefy arm under me and helped me into a sitting position. He pointed with his head. "Monty and Buck over there."

I blinked hard as I saw the two homeless guys snapping handcuffs on Troy and Joe.

"L.A.P.D.," Tracy told me. "Had their eyes on you the whole time."

If only somebody'd bothered to tell me. "My—my purse," I mumbled.

"What?"

"My purse. I shoved it through the gate back there."

"Women! You mean you made that run carrying your goddamn purse?"

I let my eyes slide shut again, which made my head hurt just a tiny bit less. "My backup tape recorder's in it, Tracy—the evidence."

"Oh."

In the next few minutes, the place was overrun with police and paramedics. There seemed to be a heated discussion amongst the cops as to whose jurisdiction took precedence. Technically, we were in Santa Monica, and that city's police were now on the scene. The "homeless guys" were Los Angeles cops. And Tracy was County. Frankly, Scarlett, I didn't give a damn who got credit for their arrests, just as long as the Palisades Playboys ended up in jail.

Two paramedics lifted me onto a stretcher and, while the police continued to battle their turf war, I found myself headed back to the emergency hospital.

12

"I want to propose a toast to Quinn," Uncle Teddy said, raising his wine glass in the afternoon sun. "May she win a Pulitzer Prize."

"Hear, hear!" said Sylvia, never one to turn down a free glass of wine. Or any other alcoholic beverage. At today's pool reopening party, she was dressed in an emerald green caftan and matching broad-brimmed sun bonnet.

"You flatter me," I said, blushing, yet feeling pretty pleased with myself. As a surprise for me, Teddy also had invited Harry and Bebe Radner from the *Star*, as well as Detective Tracy Lewis. He'd spent half the week preparing the fabulous hors d'oeuvres laid out on the poolside table. "I'll be happy if the publicity from my article gets the *Star* a few more subscribers," I added, trying to sound modest.

"Oh, we've already done that," Harry said, as if my article on the Palisades Playboys' murders had been his idea, some sort of circulation booster. "Our ad revenues are climbing nicely, too."

After leaving the emergency room nearly two weeks earlier, I'd gone home and spent most of the night rewriting my article to meet the *Star*'s weekly deadline. If I missed it, I knew every daily in town would report my story before the *Star*, and I just couldn't bear to be scooped, not on *my* story.

As a result, the *Times* picked up my piece the day after we published, giving the *Star* full credit. The *Reporter* and *Variety* did, too, although they were a bit more reluctant to cite their competition. Still, they were hard pressed not to use my name in their versions—after all, I was one of the victims. And, because of the show biz angle, even the Associated Press put my article on the wire. It got national coverage.

"Heard today there's going to be a plea bargain," Tracy informed the gathering. "At least it'll save the good citizens of California the expense of four separate trials. We had that tape Quinn made, plus those journals in Tiffany Novotny's safety deposit box. Confronted with that kind of evidence, they all started singing like choirboys, each one aiming to be first to point a finger at somebody else. Gotta give you credit, Quinn, you had the whole thing all figured out."

Because of my role in recovering the journals, I'd had the chance to read them, as long as I did so in the district attorney's office. What I'd learned filled in several holes in my story.

Rhett King had not actually witnessed the rape and murder of Lauren Hartley but, during that long night on the beach, he'd overheard his three panicky friends planning to frame Luis Alvarez for their crime. When he urged them to turn themselves in, they reacted by threatening not only Rhett's life, but his girlfriend Julia's. Rhett caved in, thus making himself part of the cover-up. As a result, he'd spent the last few years of his life feeling guilty, sinking further into drugs and despair. As he told his father all those years ago, eventually he could feel his soul bleeding.

"They confirm the blackmail scheme, too?" I asked Tracy.

He nodded. "Seems Shane ran through his brother's insurance money before he bothered to read those diaries. Once he did, he figured he'd found another gold mine.

None of his brother's buddies were in any position to pay him big bucks—they weren't rich, their parents were—but Parker Kellerman bailed them out by giving Rhett that high-ticket job at Calistoga Pictures."

"So why did they kill Shane?"

"The kid was such a disaster as a production company exec that Calistoga's CEO wanted him fired. Parker's job was on the line if he didn't get rid of Shane."

"You're not saying Parker Kellerman killed him?" Harry asked, grabbing a stuffed mushroom and popping it into his mouth.

Tracy shook his head. "No way. Parker's not the type to dirty his own hands. Quinn had it right. Stevenson Brooks scored the Rohypnol and heroin from his usual sources and gave them to Troy Kellerman and Joe Taliaferro. They went out to Shane's place, dumped some Rohypnol in the kid's beer and waited for him to pass out. After that, it was a piece of cake to strip him, carry him into the hot tub, and inject him with enough heroin to make sure he didn't wake up."

"Which is when I found him," I said, as the disturbing scene flashed through my mind.

"He'd been dead a few hours by then," Tracy said. "Those two had plenty of time to search the house. Only problem was they didn't find the journals."

"Because Shane had given them to Tiffany for safe-keeping," I said.

"He obviously didn't think she'd bother reading them."

"I can understand why," I agreed. Tiffany didn't look like a big reader. Yet she was smart enough to know these journals were worth money or Shane wouldn't have asked her to hide them, and she was definitely an opportunist.

Uncle Teddy offered more wine all around.

"After Shane was dead," Tracy said, holding out his glass, "Tiffany decided to use the journals for her own ends."

"And her goal was to be a star."

"Got that right, Quinn. Troy gave her a phony contract with his talent agency and claimed he'd signed her to star in a movie up in Big Sur. Joe posed as the director. Got her to meet him on that lonely stretch of Highway One, supposedly to check out a location. Once he had her there, he got her to share a toast to her first starring role, drugged her, put her back behind the wheel of her little car, and set it on a downhill course off the cliff. You were also right about his fingerprints being inside."

"So what's their plea bargain?" I asked, not really expecting much punishment for four rich white guys from Pacific Palisades. Now, if they'd been drug dealers from Watts or East L.A. . . .

"Twenty-five to life each for young Kellerman, Taliaferro, and Brooks. Ten to fifteen for old man Kellerman."

"Doesn't seem like much," I said, "not when you consider Luis Alvarez has already spent nearly ten years in Soledad for doing absolutely nothing wrong."

"Hey," Tracy said, palms upward. "Not my call. You ask me, I'd fry their asses, but these guys got connections and the state wants to save some bucks."

At least they would be off the streets for a good long time. Once they got to prison, I wondered how the spoiled Palisades Playboys would take to becoming rape bait themselves, instead of a bunch of rapists.

"So does this finally get Luis Alvarez released?" I asked. I'd driven up to Soledad Prison a week earlier to visit Luis, and I was impressed with how the young man had managed to cope with his nightmare. He'd helped start a prison newspaper and managed to get three of his articles on life in prison published on the Internet during his incarceration.

"That'll probably take another week or two. That lawyer of his, what's her name?"

"Madeleine Raymond," I replied. The former public defender who'd originally talked Luis into pleading guilty had finally gotten religion. Since my story appeared, she'd been doing her best to help right this old wrong, pro bono.

"Yeah, Raymond. She's applied to the Governor for a pardon for Alvarez, and the DA's concurring. Should get it in a hurry, thanks to all your publicity."

The only negative part about my recent notoriety was that Peter King was no longer speaking to me, not since I'd publicly exposed his sons' participation in blackmail and a murder cover-up. I felt bad about that, but I'd discovered my devotion to truth was far greater than my devotion to any of my old lovers. All in all, not a bad discovery to make. It would probably save me many a future heartache. I turned to Harry. "With all these new subscriptions and the extra ad revenue we're getting," I asked, "can we afford to hire a junior reporter?"

"I—I don't know. Why?"

"I want to hire Luis Alvarez, at least part time."

Harry's jaw dropped. "Why?"

"Because the kid shows real promise as a writer and he deserves a break. You know as well as I do, it's going to be hard for him to get a job after all that time in prison, even if he was never guilty."

Harry stared hard at me. "What are you up to this time?"

I did my best to look innocent. "We can use the help, can't we? If we've got more ads coming in, that means we've got more editorial space to fill, right?" I didn't mention that Luis looked plenty young enough to infiltrate the Hollywood drug club scene and help me report on it. Unlike me, this good-looking youth wouldn't be suspected of being a narc or somebody's parent. Maybe I'd be able to do my drugs-in-Hollywood story after all.

"We'll see," Harry said.

I took that as a yes.

"Don't know about anybody else," Uncle Teddy said, whipping off his terrycloth robe, "but now I've got my pool back, I'm going for a swim."

He cannon-balled into the water, suddenly looking more like seven years than seven decades old.

"Why not," I said, shedding my own robe and walking over to the edge of the pool. It felt like the right time to jump back in.

I held my nose and took the plunge.